KILLING
THE
SECOND
DOG

MAREK HLASKO

Translated by
TOMASZ MIRKOWICZ

Introduction by
LESLEY CHAMBERLAIN

NEW VESSEL PRESS
New York

KILLING THE SECOND DOG

 New Vessel Press

www.newvesselpress.com

First published in Polish in 1965 as *Drugie zabicie psa*
Copyright © 2014 Andrzej Czyzewski
Translation Copyright © 2014 New Vessel Press
Introduction Copyright © 2014 Lesley Chamberlain

Library of Congress Cataloging-in-Publication Data
Hlasko, Marek
[Drugie zabicie psa. Polish]
Killing the Second Dog / by Marek Hlasko; introduction by Lesley Chamberlain; translation by Tomasz Mirkowicz.
p. cm.
ISBN 978-1-939931-11-5
Library of Congress Control Number 2013948714
I. Poland—Fiction.

Introduction

WHEN THE POLISH-BORN WRITER MAREK HLASKO'S FIRST SHORT novel was published in 1957 he seemed to spring from nowhere. The post-war order, particularly in communist Poland, was a painful and bewildering experience for the rising adult generation. Suddenly the gutsy, pared-down, and hardly optimistic narrative of his debut novel *Eighth Day of the Week* expressed what young people felt, and how they saw their defeated, deadbeat elders. Hlasko often hinted that he never meant to be a writer, and yet, from the other side of Europe, he fit Jean-Paul Sartre's definition of contemporary style almost exactly. For the French philosopher the literary scene was now markedly under the influence of "the American writers, Kafka and Camus." Hlasko wrote in this contemporary style seemingly without trying. How he found overnight success in Poland and then worldwide is a remarkable and tragic story.

He was born in Warsaw in 1934. His father was a lawyer and his mother had artistic leanings. They divorced when Hlasko was three and in 1939, just a couple of weeks into the Second World War, his father died. In *Killing the Second Dog* the protagonist calls his father gentle and good and notes that he was killed fighting the Germans. Perhaps we can take that as an indication. Certainly it's the nearest to an autobiographical account we have. Hlasko's mother ran a grocery stall in the capital during the Nazi occupation, but when the 1944 Warsaw Uprising failed, she and her son fled, along with thousands of others, to safer parts of the country. In his 1966 autobiography, *Beautiful Twentysomethings*, Marek remembered, aged ten, starting a new life in Czestochowa, southwest Poland. Shortly afterwards his mother remarried, and the family moved to Wroclaw, the nearest larger city. Thanks in part to his mother urging the poets upon him, the boy excelled in composition, but otherwise his school career was stormy. Several times expelled for aggressive behavior, he had his first taste of manual work at age thirteen. At sixteen he was a truck driver, an experience which formed the basis for a hair-raising account of real working conditions under post-war communism, *Next Stop Paradise*, written some years later.

A brief return to formal education was formative. In Wroclaw around the age of fifteen Hlasko attended the Vocational Theater School. Courses intended to turn out back-stage professionals introduced him to dramatic writing, and gave him contact with film and filmmakers. He began to read, not least the great playwrights, and to write. Meanwhile on the strength of his laboring background in 1951 the Communist Party newspaper *Tribuna Ludu* hired him as a "people's reporter." The task in communist days for all writers was to deliver a glowing account of working-class valor and virtue, but when Hlasko's first stories appeared in 1954 they portrayed disillusioned, drink-sodden, malicious lives. Here was a world in which youthful idealism was soon shattered. After Soviet dictator Joseph Stalin died in 1953, the whole East Bloc heaved a sigh of relief that the bitter truths of everyday life could once again be told, although the message took a while to filter through to cautious cultural bureaucrats. When in 1956 the new Soviet Communist Party leader Nikita Khrushchev openly denounced his predecessor, that was the first intentional signal of a great easing-up. Hlasko's debut collection of stories *First Step in the Clouds* appeared. And yet, by 1957, when that collection won the prestigious Publishers' Prize, the ideological chill was back. The frankness of *Eighth Day of the Week* became was an embarrassment and work on turning it into a film was abruptly curtailed, pending radical changes.

Perhaps no writer from those times in any East Bloc country has left such a detailed account, in his autobiography and scattered through *Killing the Second Dog*, of what that swift change in 1957-58 meant to a young writer who was lionized and ostracized in quick succession. Hlasko's headstrong and vulnerable character, and a proud belief in his work, put him on a collision course from which he was never able to recover.

When a decade later Hlasko's work began to appear in English, foreign critics pounced on a writer who with his matinee good looks resembled James Dean's Rebel Without a Cause and sounded like one of Britain's Angry Young Men, impatient with lack of opportunity in a stultified class society after the war. But because of what he had witnessed under the Nazi occupation, and what communism brought to Poland, Hlasko was a rebel, and a writer, of quite a different order, one whom non-Polish readers perhaps can only begin to understand with hindsight.

The ideological upheaval of 1958 meant that Poland's submission at the Cannes Film Festival was canceled. It was to have been the film version of *The Eighth Day*. While a toned-down version eventually materialized, Hlasko was bitterly disappointed. Meanwhile Polish publishers rejected his two latest fictions, *Next Stop Paradise* and *The Graveyard*. A state-sponsored writers' visit to France, intended to make Polish names better known in the West, did go ahead, and Hlasko took part, with, amongst others, the poet and future Nobel laureate Wislawa Szymborska. But quietly at this point the state seems to have decided to cut its ties with Hlasko. He was allowed to leave the country, but without the funds he needed to live on in Paris. In those Cold War days when an official patriotism was required of every citizen, Poland had a reason for not wanting back this novelist who wrote of life there as grim and cheap. When he secured a French publisher for his rejected titles he gave them an even better one, in those crazily ideological days: an apparent lack of patriotism.

Hlasko decided to put a positive spin on his precarious situation by visiting America, but with his passport about to run out he didn't qualify for a visa. Three years followed in which the communist Polish state played cat and mouse with the young man's deep emotional need to return home. They make heartrending reading in *Beautiful Twentysomethings* and again in *Killing the Second Dog*.

The unrenewed passport, exchanged for the papers of a refugee, allowed Hlasko to travel in France, West Germany and Italy. In 1959 he married the German actress Sonia Ziemann who had played the female lead in *Eighth Day of the Week*, and they lived for a time in Munich. Photographs of that marriage – and images are all we have to go on – show an attractive happy couple. Sonia liked to drive fast and Marek obliged with the car she bought him. But later in 1959 Hlasko was already alone in Israel, ostensibly invited by friends, actually looking, illegally, for work.

In Israel he hoped those friends could help him. Polish Jews who had fled anti-Semitism, German Jews who had survived the war, and Jews already born in Israel, were now his compatriots and his "family." In *All Backs Were Turned*, set in 1961, at a time when in Europe the Berlin Wall was going up, and in *Killing the Second Dog*, Hlasko would vividly evoke the tough, brazen, deeply unfriendly Israeli milieu in which he found himself. In staggering heat he was forced for a while to work in a blast furnace. When his wife came to find him someone stole the razor and towel that were his only possessions, as he turned his attention away from his place on the beach. The style of his Israeli novels, written between 1961 and 1966, seemed to combine hard-boiled American crime with biblical simplicity. *Killing* mentions St. Paul and Mickey Spillane almost in the same breath. Perhaps Hlasko felt some affinity with a persecuted people starting afresh in a new homeland. The condition of a relatively new Israel was a replica on a grand scale of his own disturbed life. But he made clear his feeling that so many millions, not only Jews, had suffered. In the four short novels and several short stories he set in Israel it was not hope for one people, but the impossibility of human goodness as such, which obsessed him.

In Czestochowa in 1945 he witnessed the arrival of the Red Army to "liberate" the city. Terrible memories from that time come back to haunt the protagonist of *Killing the Second Dog*. In his autobiography Hlasko remembered the woman who tried to avoid being raped by addressing the commandant in Russian and welcoming him with a shot of vodka. The glass was trampled underfoot. The Russian spoken by soldiers violating a man's wife came back verbatim: "Don't worry, we'll just give her a little poke and then it's over." These nightmares merged with bad conscience at what the penniless immigrant without work was forced to do to survive in Israel. There is poignant moral desperation in Hlasko, as readers of *Killing the Second Dog* will find.

A photograph of Hlasko still in Israel after two years shows him bitter and worn-down at not yet thirty. From Israel where he labored in Tel Aviv, Eilat and Jaffa, he begged the Polish authorities to allow him home. Like the protagonist of *The Graveyard*, and implicitly like Kafka's Josef K, Hlasko would have been content to be judged, rather than left to wander in a living hell of absurdity and exclusion.

One feature of his writing is a contempt for religious and ideological convictions acquired, as it were, without thinking. His communist experience made him despise men and women willing to "learn how to think." *The Graveyard* studied with a pity rare in Hlasko the downfall of an official on whom the system suddenly turns, when before he had embodied that system. It was a tale which Hlasko knew bore obvious comparison with Arthur Koestler's far better-known *Darkness at Noon*.

Not ideology but the simple terrible business of how people live together hovers over the unhappy stories Hlasko tells us. In communist Poland lives were uncomfortable, downtrodden and merciless, a cruelty exacerbated by the biting cold of winter, although occasionally, for moments, the misery was redeemed by the beauty of the mountains. In Israel it was the heat, unbearable for European immigrants, and the maddening dry wind, that enveloped his characters in existential languor. The seaside settings for *Killing* and *All Backs Were Turned* have to remind us of Meursault, Camus's anti-hero in *The Outsider*, blinded by heat and light just before he shoots dead an innocent man on an Algiers beach. Civilized life struggles to come to terms with Meursault's motivation, or lack of it. In one of its aspects *Killing the Second Dog* presents a kind of absurdist tableau to a sympathetic American visitor, to win her sympathy. Perhaps the last possible way to trump the malign world is to take the absurdity of evil to new heights. Over and over situations arise in Hlasko in which characters must undermine and destroy their neighbors, or succumb themselves. Love and lust, indecipherable the one from the other, and the need to survive, drive them on. Alcohol, sleeping pills and amphetamines, and an addiction to brawling, help one day turn into the next.

All the parallels suggested by Sartre's insightful definition of the post-war novel can be followed up in Hlasko's case. Like most dissenting writers in the communist era, he was well aware that Kafka had gone before him in capturing the absurdity of the system which gave no answers and provided no entrances and exits to the mystery it seemed to enshrine. It's possible Hlasko never read Camus, but he must strike us as an existentialist writer out of sheer personal experience of being a radical outsider. In his readiness to fight back on the page against a raw deal from life he also found natural brothers-in-arms in the American writers, though no specific one comes to mind. He gives the impression of having read pulp fiction rather than Faulkner. Moreover, although early critics mentioned Hemingway, that connection seems misleading, for certainly Hlasko's world is macho, but it is hardly crowned by honor.

The plot of *Killing the Second Dog* is fraud. Two penniless immigrants defraud wealthy American women visiting post-war Israel. The ruthless Robert is the brains behind the scam, and Jacob, one of Hlasko's alter egos, is the means. The scheme plays on this other-Hlasko's good looks and his ability to learn a part. He tells these women what they want to hear. Robert in his previous life produced Shakespeare. Now he scripts scams featuring his hunky friend.

As scene follows scene, *Killing the Second Dog*, a picaresque tale of how the scheme doesn't follow the plan, derives its depth from an almost comic unwillingness to concede some genuine human emotions. The pseudo-romantic hero Jacob is at once a puppet, where he should be a human being, and a kind of Macbeth, being urged on by the ruthless Robert to do the deed, which he both does and does not.

In fact all of Hlasko's themes, bar the Israeli setting, were already evident in his first work. They include a general distrust of women and a tendency to see them as either whores or, occasionally, angels. The sex in Hlasko is mostly prostituted. Sex, in the tainted reality that destroyed a young couple's happiness in *First Step in the Clouds*, has become for men and women equally just another means to survival. Male companionship, the redeeming feature of *Next Stop Paradise*, returns in *Killing* as a something-better-than-nothing, a joint conniving, a physical dislike, but still better than being alone. Telling his unfortunate tales Hlasko excels at the one-line putdown, the witty repartee. He also memorably evokes natural forces as the backdrop to the human drama. Darkness is one theme in *Killing*. Under its unfriendly spread, the two conspirators seem to be in a tussle with the universe. The power of the sea to create a narcotic oblivion is another. "No wise-ass bastard can change that, or try to; that's what felt so good about looking at the sea."

The dog in *Killing the Second Dog* is part of the absurd show the fraudsters put on to woo their victim. Hlasko gave some half-convincing answers to curious critics at the time, including that he had once seen a Nazi shoot a dog. But in a more satisfying hermeneutic reading of the text the dog stands in for the unnamed protagonist who sacrifices the best part of himself to pull off a mean trick. Robert and partner buy only purebred, "film star" dogs, whose food costs them far more than what they spend on themselves. "The dog has to be big, happy and full of life. It's got to be loved and pampered by everybody." The gorgeous dog, whom other characters quickly love, becomes then one more pawn to manipulate in the game.

Another account of the dog suggests itself. Could it be that Hlasko, who assimilated biblical stories in his child-hood, and had his alter ego explain himself as a Catholic in *Killing*, knew the story of Tobias and the Angel? The only dog mentioned in the entire Bible accompanies the Angel who in turn accompanies Tobias on a long journey to recover his father's money. A trusted third party is keep-ing it safe. "Tobias and the Angel," in which two men set out with a dog, is a story of decency and love from start to finish, the very opposite of the world Marek Hlasko en-countered.

Yet another interesting character in *Killing* is the child, Johnny, a tough guy and a troublemaker suffering from not having a father. In his relationship with the hunky con-man from Poland we can see Hlasko the child meeting Hlasko the man. The submerged moral themes make *Killing* worth several readings. When the narrative ends with a cry for the possibility of goodness in a man's life, it is a moment for the reader to reflect on that other great influence on Hlasko's moral outlook, Dostoevsky.

After leaving Sonia Ziemann – whom uncharitably he called naïve, but of whom he also wrote that he did not want to spoil her life – a second time, Hlasko unsuccessfully tried to kill himself in Munich. Pages of his autobiography, written after he recovered from this suicide attempt, are devoted to a sarcastic account of the interview he has with a German doctor, in which he tries to tell him that the memory of what happened – with the Nazis, with the Red Army – just won't leave him.

In 1966 some promise appeared on the horizon. His old friend from Warsaw, Roman Polanski, now a successful film director in America, invited him across the Atlantic. Polanski, already famous for *Knife in the Water*, was beginning to work on *Rosemary's Baby*. With access to Hollywood and a new circle of Polish-speaking friends Hlasko had his best chance yet to start again. He was of the same traumatized generation as Polanski, who though he was born in France had grown up in Poland from the age of three and survived the Holocaust there. Both of Polanski's Jewish parents had died in Nazi death camps. In *Knife in the Water* one can see perhaps that sense of life as a barely concealed existential duel, between one man and another, over who has the possessions and the power; and where, differently, happiness might lie. A special joy for Hlasko was his friendship with the composer Krzysztof Komeda, who had written the music for *Knife in the Water* and was a key member of Polanski's team. Yet it seems that Hlasko, by the time he reached America, was emotionally so extremely fragile, the result of all he had seen in wartime Poland, and all that happened to him after, that even in happier circumstances he could barely cope without alcohol.

One night he and Komeda were so drunk that Komeda fell into a ditch and cut his head open. Trying to help him Hlasko himself fell and may have worsened the injury. Komeda recovered, only to succumb to a blood clot on the brain five months later. Apparently, this was the last loss Hlasko could endure. Perhaps with his grief compounded by guilt, he killed himself in June 1969 with an overdose of pills in a hotel in Wiesbaden, at last enacting for real the suicides his alter ego had faked in the fraud plots of *Killing*, and making up for the Munich failure six years earlier. He had been on his way back to Israel via West Germany, shuttling between countries. He was, aged 35, a man without friends, without money, without a home. Life was unbearable.

The world lost Marek Hlasko early. Polanski, the same generation and long since an international figure, and Marek Nowakowski, the comparatively obscure prose writer who remained in Poland and managed to write through the communist era despite the hurdles put his way, are, for the sake of comparison, still alive. Hlasko became so famous in such a short time, and yet nothing could compensate for the damage life did to him. He was a child and a young man in an age which had almost abandoned humanity. The feelings of displacement and loss were overwhelming.

Hlasko was first translated into English in the late 1950s, reflecting the West's eventual reception of works published during the East Bloc thaw that followed Stalin's death, and again in the early 1990s, after communism collapsed and the world had free access once more to cultures that had been locked away behind the Iron Curtain. After two cycles of interest in his work the latest rediscovery of him simply reflects the unique quality of his prose. In tune with the writerly spirit of the times that Sartre identified, Marek Hlasko created an anguished post-war literature all his own.

Lesley Chamberlain

THE RIDE FROM HAIFA LASTED OVER TWO HOURS. ABOUT halfway to Tel Aviv, we realized that the man sharing the rundown cab was in a bad way. The driver said we would soon reach the outskirts of the city and stepped on the gas, taking each turn with a screech of wheels that made us feel like actors in some B-grade movie. At one point a cop raised his hand to stop us, but the driver didn't slow down. In the rear-view mirror we saw the cop turn to his Harley standing in the shade, but he just shook his head; it was too hot to bother. He stood in the middle of the road, took off his helmet, and started wiping the sweat off his forehead.

"How is he?" the driver, without turning around, asked.

"Almost gone," Robert said and then looked at me. "Now he'll have lots of quiet and plenty of shade. Think he'll like it?"

"Do you know him?" the driver asked.

I had to hold our dog by the collar; he was fidgeting and growling. The dying man must have made him nervous. "No," I said.

In Tel Aviv the stranger died as soon as the three of us carried him out of the cab. He was lying stretched out on a bench while we waited for an ambulance. Some decent soul placed a photo magazine over his face. It had the picture of an actor on the cover; his blue eyes watched us with a piercing stare. Robert lifted the magazine and peered at the dead man's face.

"I think he was Romanian," he said. "Just arrived from Europe. He didn't speak a word of Hebrew."

"He won't have to learn it now."

"This is a bad sign."

"You mean him?"

"What else?" Robert said. "I'm superstitious. This may spoil the whole deal for us. We should've taken the train."

"Poor fellow, he's not buried yet, and he's already made another enemy."

"That's right," Robert said. "I hope they stick the bastard in a coffin and bury him deep." He looked at the driver, who was leaning over the corpse, trying to recognize the actor on the magazine cover. "We're leaving, buddy. Haven't got much time."

"It's John Wayne," the driver said finally, lifting his head. "Can't you wait a bit longer? You know how it is with the cops. They always think everything happened different than you tell them. You'd be doing me a real favor."

"We have some business to take care of," I said, "but we'll be staying at a hotel across the street. Fifty-six Allenby. If the cops ask about us, give them our address."

"Oh, they'll ask for sure," the driver said, again leaning over the corpse. "No, I guess it wasn't John Wayne I saw in *Pursued*. Must've been some other guy."

We crossed the street and walked into our hotel. The desk clerk was sitting at the end of the lobby, reading a book. I thought of the dead man and glanced at the cover that showed some guy murdering some broad, or maybe it was the other way around.

"Had a nice trip?" the desk clerk asked.

"It lasted over two hours," I said. "And some fellow we didn't know who was riding with us died right there in the cab. He was leaning against Robert the whole time."

"Stupid bastard," Robert said. "And a bad sign if I ever saw one. Have you got two beds for us, Harry?"

The desk clerk didn't answer. He kept on reading. I glanced again at the lurid cover.

"For ready cash," Robert added.

The desk clerk finally put the book down. "How long

do you want to stay?"

"We don't know yet," I said. "We came here to make some cash. That's why Robert's sore. He's convinced the corpse might mess things up."

"Are you going to try to marry him off again?" the desk clerk asked Robert.

"Sure. Hasn't it worked before?"

The desk clerk looked at me closely. "He's old. And he looks goddamn tired."

"Don't worry about me, Harry," I said. "Leave it to Robert. He knows how to make those broads part with their money."

"Sure, I know," Robert said. "The main thing is to have an idea. And I've still got lots of ideas for this guy."

"He is *old*," the desk clerk insisted.

"Leave it to me. I know best. His gloomy face is still worth its weight in gold. So, have you got those two beds or haven't you?"

"You'll have to pay for the dog, too. Hotel rules."

"We already paid once. When we bought it."

"How much?"

"Almost a hundred pounds. It's a purebred. Did you think we got it for free? And with a nanny to take it out for walks? You didn't think that, did you?"

"You'll have to pay in advance," the desk clerk said. "Four pounds. And I don't want to see that dog running around the hotel."

"The dog is always with us," I said. "Goes wherever we go. We have no secrets from it."

The desk clerk looked at me again. I knew he wanted to give me a nasty smile, but it didn't come off. His face barely twitched. The day was too hot.

"Some day you'll overdose and that'll be the end of you," he said to me. "You barely made it last time. They had to give you oxygen. I thought you were a goner."

"That's because I hadn't eaten a decent supper. Anyone

can make a mistake, Harry."

"But you already made one in Jerusalem," he said. "They had to lock you up in a psychiatric ward afterwards. Room fourteen."

I went over to the board and got our key. "I collected a whole bundle that time in Jerusalem."

"You are old." He picked up his book and turned around to put our money away. He placed the bills in a desk drawer which he left half-open, too lazy to shut it properly. "What time will you be back?"

"Before midnight," I said. "We'll just take a quick shower now and be off."

"Have you got your own towels?" Harry asked.

"No," I said.

"Two towels ... that'll be half a pound extra."

"Half a pound won't make us broke," I said.

Harry pulled two towels from the drawer. I took them, but Robert grabbed one and gave it back.

"One is enough," he said.

"Frankly, I'd prefer to have my own towel," I said.

"You'll have to learn how to save on little things," Robert said. "Otherwise you'll never get rich. I read the other day Chancellor Adenauer demanded he get paid for a TV interview, took the money from the reporter, and pocketed it right there, right there while eight million Germans watched. You should learn from him."

We walked down the dark hallway. A hunchback was sitting at the far end, reading a book. I made out his face in the slanting rays of a dim light bulb. It had that fake sweet and painful look that cripples often have. I glanced at the book he was reading, *The Life of St. Paul of Tarsus.*

"A fellow Catholic," I said. "Though not for any idealistic reason, I assume. And a hunchback at that."

"I converted to Catholicism because the priests promised to help me get a Canadian visa," the hunchback explained. "What's new? You still alive?"

"Don't worry about me," I said. "And you, I see, are still sitting in front of the john, huh? Nothing's changed, has it?"

"Well, I feel safer here," he said, pointing at the toilet door. "If I get the runs, it's only one step away. Anyway, none of your business."

"I've known this jerk for three years now," I told Robert. "And all that time he's been sitting in front of the john. Ain't he something?"

"We could use him," Robert said.

"How?"

"Oh, I'll come up with something. A hunchback has plenty of potential. But all I can think of now is taking a shower."

"Hey, blondie," the hunchback called after me, "the priests promised to give me some cash at the end of the week. Find me a broad, okay?"

"That'll cost you thirty or forty pounds," I told him.

"Why? Everybody pays twenty."

"Yeah, not everybody is a hunchback."

"They say I'll get the money when I learn the catechism. I've already memorized the Ten Commandments. Now I'm reading the life of St. Paul." He got up, his face twisted in pain. "Excuse me. I've gotta rush."

"What's wrong with him?" Robert asked.

"He couldn't stand the heat. Started drinking fresh water. It was during a khamsin that lasted for eight days. He caught some kind of stomach disease. Doctors are giving him charcoal, other stuff, but nothing seems to work. Now he wants me to find him a broad."

"I'm not surprised," Robert said. "I bet his whole sex life consists of half-assed jerking off. Let's go shower."

Shortly afterward we left the hotel and went into the nearest cafe. It was a little cooler inside; the rubber blades of an overhead fan quietly cut the air. Watching them you had the illusion of coolness. And after sixteen hours under the scorching sun, even the illusion wasn't something to be sneezed at. Robert ordered two beers, and a waiter quickly brought them to our table.

I looked at our dog. It was lying motionless, its thick paws stretched out to the side.

"He gets on my nerves," I said.

"Who? The dog?" Robert asked.

"No. Harry. The desk clerk. What does he know? Does he know how much money I made for us last year?"

"Don't give him a thought. Think of your new bride."

"Maybe he's right," I said. "I'm old. It might not work this time, Bobby. If they find me too late, that'll be it."

"No."

"You know it can happen."

"You'll be all right. Just remember to eat more beforehand. Have a big supper first. Besides, your body has built up some immunity by now."

"Don't count on it. One day it can turn out real shitty. Don't tell me you don't know that."

"Sure, it can happen," he said. "But do you know how dumb I am? I haven't even insured you. And I don't intend to take out a policy naming me as your sole beneficiary. You're not a movie star and I won't play your widow."

"Hey, I swear I never suspected you of anything like that."

"Anyway, neither of us is into this for kicks. Hell, I never expected to make my living this way. My specialty, you know, is Shakespeare. I studied English at the university so I could read him in the original. That's exactly what I'd like to be doing now."

"Let's not talk about that, Bobby."

"No, I don't mind. Did I ever tell you how I think *Macbeth* should be staged?"

I remained silent. He had told me at least a hundred times—in Jerusalem, in Haifa, during those endless trips together, and during all those nights when it was too hot to fall asleep. It was when he talked about Shakespeare that his ugly face began to light up. Now, I thought, comes the boring part.

"Did I?" he said. Shakespeare was his one true passion and like all cranks he never tired of his favorite subject.

"You did mention it," I finally said, feeling a little sorry for him. "You really are a great director, Bob. It's too bad I happen to be your only actor. And I feel pretty worthless now. My face looks lousy. I don't think the girl is gonna fall for me. Sorry, but I really don't expect it to work this time."

"It will. It will. Stop worrying. Trust me. I'll make her fall for you. Just remember this, the last time anybody called her a girl was before World War I. And stop thinking about your face. Look, it's like with Shakespeare. Shakespeare's plays shouldn't be performed. You just have to know how to say the lines. The worst thing is everybody insists on performing Shakespeare; it makes me want to puke. How can you perform a scene like the one where Hamlet and Ophelia's brother quarrel by the grave? Olivier had this brilliant idea how to perform Shakespeare, so he turned his plays into theater. Shakespeare is life, not theater."

"Don't tell that to too many people."

"I'm telling it to you," he said. "You just have to shout out your lines and walk off the stage. You don't have to perform at all. Anyway, we'll rehearse your part from the beginning."

"Tonight?"

"No. Tonight we need to rest. But first we have to talk to this backer of ours. Finish your beer and we'll go. It's cooler now." He fell silent for a moment and then asked, "What did that guy say?"

"What guy?"

"The guy in the cab. Did you understand his last words?"

"Not quite. I think it was 'pray for my soul' or something like that."

"He said it in German?"

"Yeah."

"How cliché," Robert said. "But I guess a lot of people have repeated that hackneyed phrase. Still, it's worth remembering. You can always add a word or two and change something around. I've heard that all those famous last words are a pack of lies. When Goethe was on his deathbed, they couldn't get a word out of him for posterity, so they started shining a light on his face until he finally said that famous line of his: 'More light!' Sly bastards."

"I wouldn't say a thing. I'd be too scared."

"Not even a word to the kids kneeling around your bed? Or to your wife banging her head against the floor in desperation?"

"Come on," I said. "I'm tired. Let's talk to our backer and have it over with. I want to climb into bed and sleep until morning. Look at the dog. He's beat too."

Robert paid the bill and we walked slowly toward the sea. It was already dark. I remembered reading in some book that man is but the shadow of a dream, but I couldn't think of the book's title or the name of the author. I don't know who had dropped that line on me or at what point in his life the author had written it. Was it while he was gazing at the dying flame of a candle, or watching a dog with a bone in its jaws, its eyes shining with fearful ecstasy? Or maybe it was the voice of God that had suddenly rumbled inside him and made him mutter those words while staring wide-eyed at the people around him, certain all of a sudden that he would not disappear without a trace when he reached the end of his road. And maybe it seemed to the people around him they had been allowed to glimpse some wonderful light that would never shine again. It must have been a glorious moment and I can only thank God I wasn't present, since most likely I would have added a few words and spoiled the whole show. That's the way I am. And then what would have happened to the light? But I don't like light. I like the darkness, which frees us from our faces and the shadows we cast.

"Is anything wrong?" Robert asked.

"No. I was just trying to remember something."

"And ...?"

"No luck. But don't worry. That's why I'm so fond of thinking; it doesn't lead to anything. You should know me, Robert. We've been working together for over a year."

"Ease up, man. Soon we'll start talking about money and you'll feel even worse."

"You'll do the talking."

"Right. And you just try not to have such a goddamn sad face. All you need to do is sit with us; you don't even have to listen to me. You can clean your fingernails or pick up some book and leaf through it. Don't pay any attention to what's happening. To you it should be obvious he'll give us the money. Pretend you can barely hide the boredom and disgust you feel, okay?"

"Okay," I said.

We were walking side by side. Darkness was all around us, but not the kind that envelops a city like a dream. It didn't make us forget our hot and tired bodies. This darkness was rough and hard, like the dust; and like the dust it clung to our skin.

"So, once again. How will you act?" Robert asked.

"I won't pay any attention to either of you," I said. "You won't interest me at all. I'll just sit there looking out at the garden, and your loud, repugnant voices will seem to me both meaningless and unreal."

"You got it, pal. Okay, we're here."

We entered a building and started climbing a stairway overrun by cats. It was siesta; in this country, people sleep by installments. They go to bed after coming back from work, and then again late at night. They spend their evenings in cafes or visiting friends. When you visit someone, your host usually asks whether you'd like to shower before you sit down for coffee. Robert disliked taking showers and almost always refused, claiming that only dirty people need to wash very often. *Chacun à son goût.*

Our host was sitting on the terrace, reading a newspaper. His girlfriend was sitting next to him. When she saw us, she adjusted herself in her deck chair and lowered her gaze to the floor. It was meant to show her contempt. She was putting on an act. Men look only for peace and deliverance; women have to have something churning and shifting in their lives. They're always very serious about how they feel and genuinely convinced that all those fleeting emotions they take for anger, love, or contempt are going to last forever.

"It's us, Mr. Azderbal," Robert said.

"Again?" Azderbal said.

"Didn't it work out very well last time?"

"Sure. All it took to save my neck was two top lawyers and a doctor who testified that I happen to be partially insane. I don't suppose you've come here to tell me of some new deal we could make together, huh?"

"That was an accident," Robert said. "Somebody squealed on us."

"Bullshit," Azderbal said. "I'm not interested in any more shaky deals."

I moved away and sat down on a deck chair next to the girl. She glanced at me in a brief, detached way. I could swear she'd been practicing that look in front of a mirror for the past three months, certain I was going to show up at any moment. But I hadn't shown up; I had come only now with Robert because we were short of cash. I sat next to her, staring out at the dark garden, while behind our backs the two men continued their loud conversation.

"I need money," Robert was saying. "I have to pay for his hotel, food, and all the rest."

"And for the doctor," the other added.

"Yeah, for the doctor, too. We need money for at least two, three weeks. He must have a room and three meals a day; breakfast, lunch, and dinner. He must be able to afford cigarettes, coffee, a deck chair at the beach, and a haircut and shave once in a while for him to look all right. And our dog, too, our dog costs a pretty penny."

"What does it eat?"

"Two pounds of pork a day," Robert said. "Or do you expect me to cook grits for it in my hotel room and mix them with canned kosher meat? Do you really? Well, maybe you'd eat that mush, but not this dog."

"It's too big. You should have bought a smaller dog, a poodle or a Pekingese; this one's not a dog, it's a monster, a fiend. No wonder it's so expensive to feed."

"Why don't you just say outright that we should use a dead dog? That would come out cheapest. You don't know how to make money because you don't know what investing is all about. You want a hundred percent profit on every lousy deal you make; you haven't learned that some of the best deals ever made often involve just fractions of one percent. You think like a small-scale herring merchant who has to make a hundred percent profit on every sale or else he'll die of hunger."

"You should have bought a smaller dog," Azderbal insisted.

"Don't teach me, Mister. The dog has to be big, happy, and full of life. It must be loved and pampered by everybody. People must want to feed it chocolates, while it knows it can't accept even one piece. Not even sniff it! That's what I call a real dog. A dog like that becomes an issue. And then we have the makings of a tragedy. Don't you see that? The dog must have honey-colored stars in its eyes." Robert came up to me and paused behind my chair; he was furious and awe-inspiring. "I have to tie the wings of my soul while he begrudges me a bit of meat for the dog."

"He's a jerk," I said quietly, without turning my head.

This was how we had planned it; I was to show the backer we despised him and his money, so he would think we had other options and that we came to him only because he lived so close. Azderbal and the girl twitched nervously. I continued to stare into the darkness.

"Why don't you try it yourself?" Robert asked him. "Then you'll see how difficult it is. You'll see what these women are really like. All those old bitches out to save their lives. He suffers with them and pretends to be their savior. Two lonely hearts scarred by life and all that stuff. Try doing that yourself! You don't want to? I'd like to see a woman give you forty piastres for a bus ride. Once I've seen that, I can lie down in my grave and die in peace. I'd know I hadn't wasted my life."

Azderbal looked at me. "He's too old. He's got the saddest kisser the world has seen since the death of that saint who used to sit on a pillar. What was his name?"

"St. Simeon the Stylite," I said, which was a mistake on my part; I was supposed to remain silent throughout.

"Yeah, that's the one," Azderbal said. "What does he do with them in bed? They just cry together, or what?"

"We'll divide the money three ways," Robert said. "Like we did last time."

"How much do you think it'll be?"

"I don't know. Maybe six hundred, maybe eight."

"He'll never score that much," Azderbal said, looking at me. "His face is perfect for playing poker, but not for this kind of game. Either you're blind, Robert, or else you don't want to see this. Maybe you feel pity for him and don't even know it. I can't help you."

"But he's already made a pretty bundle this way," Robert said.

"He's finished, and you simply can't see that. He's done this trick a few times too many and everybody knows about it. Why don't you find some handsome young fellow and bring him here? Then we might work something out. But don't expect me to stake my money on this one." He turned to the girl. "What do you think?"

"He's too old," she said. "He's finished. What woman wants a guy who's over thirty and looks ten years older? Women know a man like that's never going to let them change him. And that's all they ever really want."

This was her way of getting even with me for having walked out on her two years earlier. She'd been waiting ever since for a chance to take her revenge and was probably feeling disappointed that she couldn't do anything more to hurt me.

"Okay," I said. "Let's go." I got up from the chair and shook hands with Azderbal and then with her. I added in a friendly voice, "Maybe we'll make some other deal together, Azderbal."

"If it's worth my time, you can always count on me," he said.

"And how do you find her?" I asked, stroking the girl's face. "Has she learned to fake orgasms yet? She used to be rotten at that. Most likely because she has no sense of rhythm. Most women are deficient in this respect. Good night."

We left.

"Azderbal is a thief," Robert said.

"All Azderbals are thieves," I replied.

"The most thievish family of Azderbals used to live in Wroclaw," Robert said. "If they didn't swindle someone at least once a month, they'd be so depressed they'd need a shrink. Some of them even got suicidal."

I didn't answer. We walked back along the same street in silence. It was only when we were back in our hotel room that Robert finally spoke: "Don't worry, tomorrow I'll find us another backer. We don't need a lot of money. Just enough for a few days." He looked at the dog, which was lying stretched out on the floor, its red tongue hanging out. "But we do need it. There's no way we can cut our expenses any further. No one mourns a Pekingese. Or a pug. Your dog has to capture the minds of all who see it. Otherwise there'll be no tragedy."

"Have you seen her yet?" I asked.

"I don't need to. They don't differ much from each other." He moved to the window and stood there, gazing out; I looked at his white body gleaming with sweat, and the sight made me feel queasy. I wished there were a painting or a photograph hanging in the room. Anything you could fix your eyes on. But there was nothing. Only the bare walls, Robert, and the dog. I couldn't look at the dog. "Yes," Robert said, "they really don't differ. All those lonely women getting on in years who want to get married one more time. With their money, which they've been saving all their lives."

"A man wouldn't do it," I said. "You'd never find a guy who'd scrimp and save for fifteen years so that he could marry some broad he's never seen, has no idea even what she looks like. Robert, would you put your shirt on?"

"Why?"

"Your body's disgusting. God only knows why I should have to look at it."

He turned around. "That's a very good line. An excellent line. You can say it to her at some point. I'll walk off and you say, 'I've spent the best years of my life with this guy. At night I'd look at his disgusting body and think to myself that I'd never be with a woman again.' And then you take her hand and look into her eyes. Yes, that's a beautiful line. You won't forget it, will you?"

"No."

"You can even stroke her body when you say it. Though maybe not. Better not overdo things. The dialogue'll be enough."

The desk clerk came into the room. "I knew it."

"Anything wrong with knocking?" Robert said, interrupting him.

"The cops are here!" the desk clerk shouted. "Go down and talk to them. I knew something like this would happen."

I had to put my pants on again; they felt rough and hot, covered with dust. I went downstairs, but I didn't feel like walking into the street. I stood in the doorway while the policemen sat in their car and stared at me.

"You again?"

"Good evening, sergeant," I said. "Did I do anything to deserve such an unpleasant welcome?"

"Not yet. But you're going to, aren't you?"

"Gimme a break, sergeant. I'm just a sentimental guy."

"You do it again, we lock you up."

"There's no law against falling in love."

"Who's the woman?"

"I don't know. I love her is all I know. I love 'em all, sergeant. My father used to tell me when he was young he fell in love with every woman he met. I'm his spitting image. Is that so unusual?"

"You got a dog yet?"

"Would you like to see it?"

"Yeah, bring it here."

I whistled and the dog bounded down the stairs. It settled at my feet. We looked like master and best friend posing for a picture. A perfect pair.

"My god! That's not a dog, that's a horse. Where did you get it?"

"We bought it."

The sergeant turned to the other policeman. "Has anyone reported a dog missing? Check it over the radio."

While the other cop switched on his radio, I said to the sergeant, "Come on, we paid a hundred pounds for this dog."

"Does it eat a lot?"

"Sure. We feed it tripe ... and other stuff."

"You should try canned dog food," the sergeant said.

"Have you?"

"Yes, but the dog won't eat any. He's as spoiled as a movie star. We've had to cut down on our food to feed it properly. Robert's lost two pounds."

"The dog's okay," the second cop said, signing off.

"Let's go then," the sergeant said. But he kept staring at me. "I don't want any problems with you two. So be careful. Believe me, one day you and your friend'll go on a long prison diet."

"You're wrong," I said. "And besides, Robert isn't my friend. He's my manager. That's a big difference."

"Who are you then?"

"His client," I answered. "Good night."

"Good night."

They left. I turned around and went back to our room. Robert was already asleep. Lying in bed I looked again at his white body. It wasn't a pleasant sight. In a few days I'll be lying in a hospital bed, I thought, and the doctors will be fighting for my life, like the newspapers say. Will my body be as white and sweaty as his? For some reason, it didn't matter to me. I threw the sheet off. It made me feel a bit cooler, but not much. I leaned over, touched the stone floor with my hand, and put the sheet on it. Then I lay motionless, beginning to smell the stink of my own sweat. Finally, I dropped off to sleep.

I woke up some time later. Robert was sitting on the bed, smoking a cigarette.

"I can't sleep," I said.

"Me neither."

"Are you worrying about getting the money?"

"No. We'll get it tomorrow. I'm worrying about finding a kid. That's why I can't sleep."

"What do you want a kid for?" I asked. "Will you want me to feed it my own flesh like a pelican?"

"We need the kid to show what a kind-hearted man you are," he said. I could feel his irritation. He was angry that

I hadn't grasped what he had in mind right away. "She's gonna fall for it, pal. Some jerk'll start mistreating the kid and you'll be the one to stop him. Every broad has to fall for a trick like that."

"And you'll be the jerk?"

"Of course. Why waste money hiring somebody else? Don't worry, I can play the part. This is very important. It'll show you in the best light. From that moment it'll all be a breeze."

"Can't we manage without the kid?"

"I don't know," he said. "It'd be best if she had a kid of her own. With some kind of handicap. A kid with one leg shorter than the other, a hunched back, or a stammer at least. A little hunchback would be perfect. Someone gives him a kick on the butt, and you step in and act like a hero. Yeah, a sweet little cripple. Or maybe a paraplegic. Jesus Christ, think how much money we could save that way!"

"Oh, come on," I said. "Dreams like that never come true. Besides, who ever brings a hunchback to the beach?"

"Don't you worry. To you it may have a hump the size of a camel's but to its own mother the kid is as straight as the prick of a Russian soldier. What do you know about women? If they love someone, they're blind as bats."

I got up and walked over to his bed, which stood close to the window. The street outside was dark, but there was no coolness out there. The night seemed solid and dusty, like some forgotten theater set. Robert gave me a cigarette, and in the light of a burning match I saw his face was dry and tense. I thought with annoyance that he must have wiped it with our towel that was now lying somewhere on the bed.

"What's bothering you?"

"I'm worried it may not work out," I said.

"Don't be. As long as you stick with me, you'll be all right. I'm as durable as the papal state."

"Sure. But one day this con is bound to fail. We'll be the

ones to lose money. What'll you do when that happens?"

"We'll come up with some new act."

"What new act?"

"Any act. We're not any less clever than other men. We have to believe that."

"Robert, do you know what a loser is? It's a guy who keeps on losing. I'm a loser, Robert. You heard what he said: find some handsome young fellow. If you plan to go on with this hustle, one day you'll have to do just that."

"Hey, that's really good! What you said about being a loser. You have to tell her that. Say you love her, blah, blah, blah, but there's been a lot of misfortune in your life, blah, blah, until a warm female hand grasped yours, blah, blah ... It'll come out great."

"Robert, art isn't made by people working in twos or threes. Art is made by loners. That's why I used to like literature, because in literature the only ones who count for something are those who go it alone, never expecting anyone to come along one day and explain what they're really striving to achieve."

"Don't you like literature anymore?"

"No, I don't. But it's not that simple. Actually, I never really wanted to write."

"Don't think about it. Better think where we can find a kid whose sweet little looks will melt a woman's heart. A kid with eyes like diamonds. Later, we'll give him money for ice cream and he can catch dysentery for all I care. That kid has spoiled my whole night. The fucker isn't even big enough to cut himself a piece of bread and he's already a pain in the ass."

I lay down next to Robert and he moved over to the wall. We lay like that for a while, listening to the sound of our own breathing. I was sure neither of us would be able to fall asleep, but I didn't care. Looking at Robert, I knew he was thinking about the kid and that his mind was working full steam, coming up with new ideas and rejecting them one after the other. At least I could be certain tonight he wouldn't bore me with his bullshit about the kind of theater he longed to create.

"You're a loser, too, Robert."

"Not yet," he said. "Right now I'm one of those who've figured out a good angle. It was me who found you and guessed you'd once wanted to be an actor. It set me thinking and I came up with this scam. This whole thing is my baby."

"History will never forget you."

"What amuses me most," he said, "to the point that I wake up at night howling with laughter, is all those broads listening to you talk about love and the life you'll lead together. None of them ever knowing all your lines were made up by a fat old Jew suffering from a double hernia who feels sick even after eating wild strawberries with cream. And that I'm that old Jew. You do all the work while I just lie peacefully in bed and wait for the moment when you'll collect the bundle and depart in an unknown direction, whispering the most tender endearments. No, son, I'm not a loser. I'm the one who's created you and this little piece of theater."

"Sure, but one day you'll have to come up with something else. I'm sorry, but that's the goddamn truth."

"I'll make you up again from scratch. No problem."

"I could do with a drink," I said.

"Everything's closed at this hour. Think of the kid."

"I hate kids."

"So do I. All kids except this one. It'll make a neat beginning. You'll both look at the kid, then at each other, and your thoughts will rush up to the Pearly Gates."

"I don't think 'rush' is the best word," I said. "I think 'soar' has a nicer ring to it."

"Okay."

"So how should I phrase it?"

"I don't know. Maybe just say, 'Let me fly away with

you.' Don't worry. In dialogue there's no need for perfection. You have to deliver your lines slowly and in a clumsy way, forgetting that you know them by rote. You have to believe these words are your own. And she must see how hard it is for you to speak, how much trouble you have finding the right words and stringing them together. That's the way Shakespeare should be staged."

"But that's not Shakespeare," I said. "It's a line from some song."

"What is?"

"Let me fly away with you."

"What's the difference? Just don't forget what you ought to be feeling."

"When am I supposed to say that? After you act out the scene with the kid?"

"Yes. The kid is very important."

"And then will I ... you know?"

"Don't worry. I'll tell you when the time is ripe."

"Let's rehearse some more. We won't be able to sleep anyway."

"Okay." He got up from the bed and wrapped himself in a sheet. I sat and smoked.

"Where do you want to start?"

"Doesn't matter," I said. "Any place."

"All right. Let's start from when she tells you that she's got to go back to the States after her vacation."

"You first."

"I didn't want to broach this subject earlier," Robert said, "but you know I'll have to leave soon, don't you?"

"My darling, why didn't you tell me that sooner?"

"I'm only a woman," Robert said. "I wanted to be happy with you for as long as I could."

"I didn't expect the summer to pass so quickly," I said.

"I must ask you something."

"No. Please let's not talk about this. I know what you want to ask. But I can't go with you."

"Why?"

"I won't bring you luck. I'm a loser, you know. Nothing ever changes for men like me. I'd keep losing just the same on the other side of the ocean."

"Then let's try to be losers together."

"You're only a woman. And it's best to be a loser alone. It hurts less."

"Wrong," Robert said. "Your lines should go this way: 'You're only a woman so you don't believe in defeat, but I've learned the hard way what it means. It's best to be a loser alone. It hurts less.' Will you remember, please? And don't say 'It hurts less' immediately after saying 'It's best to be a loser alone.' Take a pause. You're thinking and struggling with yourself, hating your words, hating yourself for saying them. This is a dialogue, for god's sake, not a litany to Our Lady of Lorraine. These words hurt you. You have to say, 'It's best to be a loser alone,' then smile like someone who's forced to lend his sports car to his mother-in-law, and only then say 'It hurts less.' Do you see it now?"

"Yes," I said. "Let's move on to the pathetic part, okay?"

"Sure. Go ahead."

"When you're twenty years old, you're unwilling to settle for any compromise where women are concerned," I said, taking Robert's fat paw in mine. "Later, you become mature enough to accept compromise. And then one day you learn to love a woman who ..."

"Louder! You're unable to believe your own words. You feel disgusted with yourself."

"... who is far away and living with another man, but you are happy that she exists, that she's alive and breathing, and you don't care if she belongs to somebody else. You just thank God that she's alive and that you can think about her whenever you like." I fell silent; I looked at his face, and after a few seconds I looked down and saw the towel Robert had wiped himself with lying on the floor. "And that is old age, which has come upon you too fast."

"We will face it together," Robert prompted.

"One day people stop visiting you and so you start visiting them. That's the onset of old age."

"A good line," Robert said. "Where did you get it from?"

"Some movie. I think Fredric March played in it. There was also something about kids. That when you go to visit your kids who've forgotten you, you know you've turned old."

He put the sheet back on the bed. "Well, that about wraps it up. You're doing fine. Just remember not to speak too fast. Deliver your lines as badly as you can. It has to seem that all the words are your own."

"Robert?"

"What?"

"Hasn't it ever crossed your mind that these words could be my own?"

"Don't think about that. Try to imagine that I created you from scratch. Disney created Donald Duck, but he probably doesn't believe it himself anymore. Same thing with Goofy. Goofy's got his own life now. That's the way you should picture yourself."

IN THE MORNING LOUD NOISES WOKE ME UP. I PULLED ON my pants and walked into the hall. Two men were fighting; one was stretched out on the floor, the other was kicking him in the face with the point of his shoe. The fight was taking place in front of the john. The hunchback cowered in a corner, like a gloomy spider. The two men fighting bumped into me; I kicked one, then the other. Their loud cries woke up other hotel guests who poured out into the hall and pulled them apart; both men yelled for the police.

"What was that all about?" I asked the hunchback.

"Me."

"What did they want from you?"

"They wanted to touch me."

"Well, then, I guess you should have let them."

"It's not that simple. They both make deals in the city. So you see the problem."

"No, I don't."

"Both believe touching a hunchback brings luck. But only if you touch him first. That's why they were fighting. They've been fighting over me for two years now."

"And you?"

"What can I do? When things get out of control, I lock myself in the crapper and wait for the cops. They don't know the truth anyway. My hump is reserved for Azderbal. The old crook comes here every morning before going to the city and he touches me. He pays me ten pounds a month. Though today someone came even earlier and gave me a pound to let him touch first."

I looked at him. "That was Robert, wasn't it?"

"Yes. He told me he had to find a new backer. And I let him touch first."

"And you forgot to tell Azderbal about it, didn't you?"

"It slipped my mind."

Soon afterward we went to a small cafe by the sea, Robert, myself, and a man Robert had found to be our backer. He was a quiet man, not much older than me, but with the build of a professional bouncer.

"Is everything clear?" Robert asked.

"Yes."

"Okay, then give us the money. No point wasting time."

"I only said everything is clear." The bouncer shook his head. "I didn't say I'd give you the money."

"You didn't?"

"Look, I need to think it over. And listen, does that goddamn dog of yours ..."

"I've told you five times already it doesn't bite," Robert said. "A strong man like you, how can you be afraid of a dog?"

"The dog may not know if I'm strong or not," the bouncer said. "And even if it does, it can still bite me out of spite." He glanced at the dog. "Have you had a vet look him over? He's got bloodshot eyes."

"Give us the money," Robert said. "We haven't got time to argue with you."

"I have to think about it a while."

"Stop playing games," I said. "Our woman is already in the hotel, somebody making a pass at her this minute. The city's swarming with guys out to make a quick buck."

A man came to our table. I could see he'd hit the bottle real hard last night. His face was pale and swollen around the eyes, his hands shaking. He was shabbily dressed and very thin; his frayed shirt, a hand-me-down from someone much taller, hung on him like on a scarecrow. I knew right now, at nine in the morning, with the sun eating away at his eyes, he was feeling miserable.

"Buy me a beer," he said. "Some day I'll stand you one."

"Beat it," Robert said. "We're busy."

"Buy me a beer," the drunk said again. I could tell by his shrill voice he was unstable: one of those drunks who start crying after the first sip. I took out thirty piastres and handed it to him.

"Here. Go buy yourself a bottle."

"I wasn't talking to you," he said. "I was talking to him." He pointed to Robert.

"Take the money and beat it." I stretched out my hand with the thirty piastres showing, but he slapped it away and the coins fell. "That wasn't very nice," I said softly. "Leave us alone now."

This made him angry. He poked me in the chest with his finger. "So you think you're a better man than me."

"No." I got up, grabbed him by the elbow, and dragged him to the door. He tried to resist, but he was so weak I hardly felt anything. The waiters at the door took him off my hands and threw him onto the street. He fell on the pavement, unable to get up. The waiters watched with amusement.

"Don't hit him," I said.

"This is a place for respectable customers," one of them said.

"Not if I'm here." When I got back to our table, I asked the bouncer, "What's with the waiters? Why do they like to gang up on drunks?"

"You should know," he said. "You used to work as one."

"You know everything about me, don't you?"

"Only what I was able to find out," the bouncer said. "I'm the one who's financing this operation. I have to know who's working for me."

"He's not working for you," Robert said. "He's an artist."

"And how about you? You an artist, too?"

"Of course. I've always been one. Nothing can ever change that."

"Look," I said to the bouncer, "if you know so much, then you must know the guy who wanted us to buy him a beer.

"I used to."

"Who is he?"

"We were in the army together," the bouncer said, "but then his wife left him and he started drinking. He was married to some foreign woman. Now he's hit bottom. Didn't even recognize me."

"Another nut," Robert said.

"In Israel you drive past a nuthouse every two miles," the bouncer said. He and Robert continued talking, arguing back and forth really. I stopped listening. I was looking at a dark-haired girl in uniform sitting by the window; she reminded me of a girl who had once invited me to her house and whose mother had fainted when she saw me because I looked exactly like some guy from the SS who had killed her uncle and his kids and forced her to watch. The dark-haired girl paid her check and left. I thought of a man I shared a hotel room with once; he was constructing a bomb he planned to throw at the minister of finance. Since he had no experience at bomb-making, everybody was afraid to stay with him. Then I started thinking of someone else, the brother-in-law of our hotel desk clerk. When his family committed him to a mental hospital, he set the building on fire. All the nuts ran off to some nearby orange grove, dancing and singing, and the cops had to search two days for them and move them to other hospitals all over the country.

Robert left the table to make a phone call. He returned right away in the best of spirits, beaming like shit in heaven.

"Good news!" he said. "We've got a kid!"

"Where'd you find him?"

"Didn't even have to look. Your new bride's got a kid of her own. She's a divorcée." He slapped the bouncer on the arm. "This is a foolproof deal. The woman is a divorcée. No husband, a child in need of a father, and she's not so young anymore. Everything will work out just fine. Give me the money."

"Okay," the bouncer agreed suddenly. "Just write me a receipt."

"Later. When there's paper."

"Write it on a napkin," the bouncer said. Robert did, but you could tell by the drops of perspiration on his forehead that writing out receipts was not something he enjoyed. The bouncer meanwhile was watching me with the same kind of friendly interest you usually reserve for lizards and spiders.

"Don't look at me like that," I told him.

"You won't con me, will you?" he asked. He was still staring straight at me, but a helpless look had appeared in his eyes. He seemed surprised by the paper napkin. He held it gently between the thumb and forefinger of his left hand. Robert had given the napkin to him in exchange for the money.

"No," I said. "We never con a partner. You can ask anybody who knows us."

He kept holding the napkin in his hand. He stared at it for a while and then moved his gaze back to me. "Don't you ever feel sorry for them?"

"Sometimes I do. Sometimes not at all. I felt sorry for one woman. A teacher from Boston."

"Boston?"

"That's right. Name was Louisa. I got a letter from her later."

"What did she write?"

"Just one word: 'Why?' I never wrote back."

"You should have. If I were you, I would have written her."

"I don't know how to answer letters like that," I said. "Put that receipt in your pocket. If you lose it, Robert won't give you a new one. I know him pretty well."

"Right," the bouncer said. His thick fingers unbuttoned his shirt pocket and he slipped the napkin inside. His eyes were still fixed on mine and it was getting on my nerves. "Wouldn't you prefer to lead a different life?" he asked.

"I've never given it any serious thought."

He continued to stare at me with a confused and helpless look.

"Don't you like my face?" I asked. "Well, neither do I. Just imagine how nice it would be if I looked exactly like you. Neither of us would need a mirror to shave."

"Okay," Robert said. "Let's go get the bullets, then pick up his things."

"What kind of gun do you have?" the bouncer asked.

"A 9-mm pistol."

"Me, too, so you don't need to buy any ammo," the bouncer said. "Just don't tell anyone where you got it."

"Don't worry," Robert said. "We've got a gun permit. Come on, let's go pick up his things."

"Where did you leave them?"

"I never said we had them," Robert said. "You're the one who's gonna lend them to us. A suitcase, a few shirts, and so on. He can't move into the hotel naked and barefoot, can he?"

"You never told me anything about a suitcase and clothes," the bouncer said.

"I forgot. But I'm telling you now. What's the difference? Anyway, he doesn't need much. Only a couple of things. Is your mother alive?"

"Yes," the bouncer said.

"How old is she?"

"Over sixty."

"Have you got a picture of her?"

"I can find one."

"She'll be his old mother who died a year ago," Robert explained. "She had cancer, so he went heavily into debt to send her to a Swiss clinic where she was operated on by a famous surgeon. But it didn't work and she died three weeks after the operation. Her constitution was so weak she had no chance. Now she's buried in a small green cemetery and he has to pay off his debts. Do you see it now? He needs his passport to leave Israel, but his passport is in the hands of the lawyer who represents the people he owes the money to. All clear?"

"Yes," the bouncer said. "But he doesn't look at all like my mother."

"So what? Hard living has changed his looks completely. Don't worry about things like that. Leave it to us."

We went to the bouncer's house. He lived in a nice area; the windows looked out on Jaffa. We could see the white needle of a minaret and the twisting streets, and we could smell all the familiar smells: fish, grilled meat, and hot copper. While the bouncer was packing clothing into a suitcase, studying each piece separately and folding it carefully like a loving wife, I said to Robert: "You've got to stay with me, Bobby."

"Stay with you? Where?"

"At the hotel."

"Are you crazy? My being there would only embarrass her."

"No, it wouldn't. Just the opposite. Listen, I've created a role for you: you'll be my best pal, the friend who doesn't want to leave me alone in the middle of my depression. And so on."

"What do you mean, 'and so on'?"

"You know how to work out the rest."

"I don't like it," he said.

"Why not? Anyway, I don't give a shit. I don't want to be by myself. I told you I don't believe we'll succeed this time. I just don't. So I need you with me."

"What about the extra cost?"

"We'll rent the cheapest room. It won't make such a big difference. Anyway the bellhop who finds us all these broads should be able to get us lower rates. He makes something on this deal, too, doesn't he? I refuse to be alone, and that's it."

"Have you lost your self-confidence?"

"I never had any. Remember, it's you who created me. Like Disney created Donald Duck."

"No, I didn't."

"Have it your way. But if you don't come with me, I'm not going through with it. Do it yourself. You know the script. I'll visit *you* in the hospital. Maybe bring you something to read. If you're still able to read, that is."

"This is blackmail."

"It sure is."

The bouncer finished packing my suitcase. Standing in front of us, he took off his shirt and wiped the sweat off his body with it, while I watched his rippling muscles. His arm was as thick as a boa constrictor. I burst out laughing, and they both stared at me.

"What are you laughing at?" Robert asked.

"At you, Bobby. Because if this whole deal falls through, it's you who'll have to come here and explain to this guy why he won't be getting his money back. God, won't that be funny!" I got up and moved to the door. "Bring the suitcase to the hotel. I'm going to get a haircut. See you around, Constrictor!" I added, turning to the bouncer. "If this whole deal, God forbid, falls through, remember it was his idea, not mine. So don't go chasing after me with that gun of yours. And Bobby, remember to feed the dog. It hasn't eaten yet. I'll show up at two. Try to get us a room looking out at the sea, okay? I'd enjoy that."

As I was leaving, they started to argue again; the bouncer wanted to give Robert the picture of his mother without the silver frame it was displayed in. Robert insisted the frame was indispensable as additional proof of my filial devotion. He drew a vivid picture of me as a penniless beggar who nonetheless refuses to part with the thin silver frame his mother's picture is set in.

"He could have sold that frame a hundred times," Robert said, "when he was hungry or ill. But he didn't! God, you don't understand the simplest things!"

I SMOKED A CIGARETTE NEXT TO A STACK OF DECK CHAIRS guarded by a small boy and watched the woman from a distance. Our rooms were on the same floor, but she didn't know that yet; she had gone down to the beach right after lunch and was sitting there with a pile of magazines scattered around her, while her kid, a boy of ten at most, was running around like a little devil, making a nuisance of himself. She didn't look too bad; she was one of those women who got a late start in life, and her face was still young and bright. I like women with bright, innocent-looking faces like that, faces that have a nun-like air about them. These are the only faces that provide the emotions and the element of surprise that make life bearable. And that was exactly her appeal. When you wake up in the middle of the night and the cogs of your brain start turning and throttling your heart, and it's almost dawn and you know you won't be able to fall asleep again, you can screen yourself from sadness and anger with the image of a face like that. I could use her face the way a child brings up his hand to shut out the view of something he's afraid of. The boy tending the deck chairs asked me for the third time if I'd like to rent a chair. I did and strolled down to the beach with it.

I walked right up to her and set my deck chair next to hers.

"This spot vacant?" I asked. I picked up one of her magazines and studied the face of some jerk and then put it back on the sand. "I'd like to know if this spot is vacant or not," I repeated.

She looked at me and gestured at the beach, empty except for the two of us. "The whole beach is vacant," she said.

"I don't care about the whole beach. I'm asking you about this spot."

"It's not vacant now," she said. "Unfortunately."

"No need to insult me. It's standard practice when people go to dinner, they ask someone to keep their spot for them. A simple courtesy. That's why I asked. If you don't want to be disturbed, put up a sign that says so. Or bring a policeman and make him stand in the sun, protecting you."

"Have you finished?"

"No. Not yet. I'll let you know when that happens."

I placed my chair on the sand and took out a book and opened the pages at random. I wasn't reading, or, if I was, the text wasn't registering in my mind; I was wondering whether Robert would have been satisfied with my act. I felt he would. He wanted me to be aggressive. Even more than that: to be violent with a fury aimed at everything and everybody. Women didn't trust men who sat down next to them and tried to charm them right off; all the sweet talk would come later, unexpectedly, at some point when Robert gave me the cue; but first I had to display the bitterness and fury of a poor soul whom the heavens had spared no misery. It was only then that women, each and every one of them, took upon themselves the role of playing go-between in the conflict between Fate and the man they had chosen for their own, the one they would follow through fire and water, to hear the peals of golden trumpets. But nothing could be hurried, the fury couldn't disappear right away; it had to dissolve gradually, slowly quiet down, and finally die out like a fire in the tormented soul of someone who's found the ladder to heaven in a woman's gentle touch. That man was myself!

I flipped an unread page and looked over my shoulder. Robert was walking in our direction with a deck chair under his arm, his face twisted from the effort though the chair weighed no more than seven pounds. Poor Robert; he always looked like an insect emerging into light for the first time from under an overturned stone. He was pale beyond belief, and I thought of the bouncer with his brown, dry skin. Robert opened his deck chair and settled into it, breathing heavily through his mouth; then he pulled out a pack of cigarettes and handed it to me. He had scrawled on it: "An American?" I gave him a light and nodded my head. So did he; this meant that we would speak English only.

"It's a hot day," Robert said.

"Yes," I said. "How clever of you to have noticed."

"How long have you been here?"

"I went to the consulate and then came straight back. There was a goddamn crowd there."

"So you did go?"

"Didn't I say I would?"

"If you had asked me for advice ..." he began.

"But I didn't," I said, interrupting him.

For a while we smoked in silence. Some old fart and his wife had gone into the water together and were splashing at each other like a couple of kids.

"Quite a sight, huh?"

"Somebody should shave that bastard's balls and send him back to kindergarten."

"For Christ's sake," Robert said. "They're just an old couple having some fun."

"No," I said. "What they really are are mirrors you can't break. You can never break all the mirrors."

"I don't like it when you say something you don't really mean," he said. "What you just said about mirrors was very nasty. It reminds me of someone. He wasn't such a great writer as you think. And he knew it. Someone who goes hunting for forty-five years doesn't shoot himself accidentally while cleaning a rifle."

"Okay, but at least he knew the menus of all the restaurants in the world. And the prices of all the drinks. That counts for something. You probably don't even know how much a Gold Star beer costs if you drink it standing by the bar!"

"Hey, take it easy. I know you've had a hard day."

"Can I try your patience some more and ask you for a favor?"

"Yep," he said. He had always liked Gary Cooper and it came as a heavy blow to him when that handsome old fellow died. I remember the day; we went to a movie theater on Ben Yehudah Street, and it seemed hard to believe that all the life had gone out of that face brightening up the screen. The whole audience was sad and unusually quiet. I expected any moment someone would come up to me and say: "It's not true. Some goddamn drunken reporter made it up."

"What's the favor?" he asked.

"Can you help me brush up on my English, old buddy?" I said. "I've landed a job."

"You've landed a job?" he repeated in a voice full of joy. "Does this mean you won't have to leave for ..."

"On the contrary, that's where the job is. I got a letter from my friend in Australia."

"And ...?"

"I'm going."

"Oh, my god!" Robert said.

"Yep. He's found me a job in some local company. And, of course, he's sponsoring me. They've even agreed to pay my way, something they never do. I've no idea how he managed it. He's probably not only had to vouch for me, but also given them an IOU. I'll have to sign a five-year contract."

"What kind of job is it?"

"When I was in the consulate today," I said, "the officer who has been processing my application ..."

"I asked you what kind of a job," Robert broke in.

"In a mine!" I shouted in anger. "What did you expect?

That they'd ask me to head the Baptist Church in Melbourne, for Christ's sake?"

"No, I didn't. But I don't think a mine is the best place for someone whose field is eighteenth-century literature." He fell silent; I watched his face in wonder as it slowly turned toward the woman. God, he was absolutely great: the dismay and shock he wanted somebody to witness and his confidence as an actor were truly incredible. Looking straight into her eyes, his face transfixed with horror, he said to me, "You, a specialist in literature of the Enlightenment, to work in ..." and then he stopped, unable to go on, as if suddenly he seemed totally helpless and everything was unworthy of words.

Now it was my turn to be silent for a while, so that his words would have time to sink in. Finally I glared at him, and, remembering to speak softly, asked, "Do you think I had any choice?"

He turned to her much more swiftly than you would expect, considering his bulk, and slowly unclenched his fist. In the middle of his sweaty palm lay a crushed booklet of paper matches. You crush matches like that unconsciously, in a spasm of internal anger. "Do you have ...?" he mumbled and broke off.

"A light?" she asked.

"Yes." He took the lighter she gave him and lit a cigarette. But he didn't return the lighter to her at once; he sat squeezing it tightly in his sweaty hand, staring straight ahead as if he'd suddenly gone blind. He was pretending to be utterly shocked by my decision, even though what I said was the text he had prepared for me.

"Give the lady back her lighter," I said. The sound of my voice brought him back to life. He returned the lighter, and although I couldn't see his face, I knew it was filled with shame and embarrassment.

"I'm very sorry," he said.

I glanced at her; her face also reflected embarrassment

at having overheard our conversation; and I could see pity in her eyes.

"Don't be," she said. She smiled, and it was at that moment that something Robert calls the invisible bond of friendship joined our hearts together.

He turned to me with a crazy look on his face, a look that was the natural reaction to the sight of a gentle and sad feminine face.

"Now you want me to teach you English," he said in a high shrill voice. "Me, the guy who has gone over the whole of Elizabethan literature with you, who has even translated Macbeth's monologue for you."

"That won't be useful to me anymore," I said. "And please, stop shouting. They aren't going to pay me for knowing Shakespeare, but for pushing wagons of coal. Or whatever else the job demands."

"What about your future?"

"My future? That's a word I won't be needing anymore."

He jumped up from his chair and stood in front of me. "Why don't you just kill yourself?" he said, his fat lips quivering. "Don't you think it would be better for you?"

Hearing this, I stood up also. "I didn't ask you for advice. When the time comes, I'll know what to do. Right now all I want from you are a few hundred measly words which come in handy."

I gave him a violent push and walked away, my back and shoulders shaking with emotion. I dived into the sea and swam around for a while. The water was still warm, but you could feel that in an hour or so the evening cool would come and give the sweltering city a moment's grace. I thought of what Robert was doing now, thought of him just getting up from the sand. I didn't have to to turn around: I knew the script.

"I'm very sorry," Robert says. "I've never seen him so upset."

"Has something happened?"

He gives her a dead stare. He doesn't understand the question.

"Has something happened?" she asks again, her voice tremulous.

"I thought you heard," he says.

"Your friend is planning to go away?"

"He isn't planning, he's made up his mind. This is the worst thing that could happen. You know, he belongs to a dying species. He's one of the few who always do what they say. Poor fool, he doesn't even know how unfit he is for surviving in this world."

"Aren't you exaggerating?" she asks. "Being a miner isn't the end of the line, you know. One of my cousins ..."

"He's not one of your cousins!" Robert shouts, interrupting her rudely. He is angry at her for not being able to grasp the simplest facts. "You don't know what a fool he is. For five years, while studying for his degree, he worked nights as a cab driver to support himself. He studied literature. His father was a tyrant who didn't want him to study and refused to help him even once during all that time. And yet when he got his degree, he came back home and said to his father ... You know what he said?"

"What?" she asks.

"Well, he said, 'Dad, I ...'" And then Robert falls silent and just waves his hand. It's not even a wave, just a shadow of that gesture, signifying utter dejection.

"Come on, what did he say?" she asks.

"Forget it. It doesn't matter now, does it? Did you hear what that fool said about his future?" Robert is mocking me now, but in the way you mock someone you love deeply. "'Future's a word I won't need anymore.' Shit! The worst thing is I believe him. I believe him because nobody knows him like I do."

And that poor sad cunt will never know what I said to my tyrant of a father, who sometimes was a lawyer and sometimes a doctor; for the cunts from New York he was a lawyer, for the ones from California a doctor. Or maybe the other way around. It's unimportant. The beautiful thing is, she'll never know what I said. And Robert doesn't know either, but he's taught me to appreciate the power of an unfinished conversation, which can be resumed naturally and easily after a few hours or even a few days. My real father was a good and gentle man who died when I was six. But a father like that was absolutely worthless, Robert said. "Forget him. Your father has to be straight out of a Dickens novel. Maybe even a religious fanatic who drove your mother to an early grave. Leave your parents to me." I soon learned one of my uncles was a madman who had murdered his wife in a sudden attack of jealousy, that my parents were both alcoholics, and later—this was when we were hustling the girl from Boston—that I didn't have a father at all but was the illegitimate son of a poor washerwoman who knew nothing about my father except that he was a corporal on summer maneuvers with his regiment. "The unfortunate child grew up unwanted like a weed and a sore in everybody's eye," Robert told the poor bitch, pointing at me. Both of them had tears in their eyes.

I dived into the water a couple more times and then went back to where they were sitting.

"I'm sorry," I said to Robert. "I shouldn't have said that."

"It's okay. You don't have to apologize. I'm your friend, you know," he added after a pause.

I looked at him and smiled sadly, the way you smile when you feel like crying, and Robert answered me with the same kind of smile: there was no strength in it, only the loyalty of one beaten man to another. This was one of those moments when people feel that something special is happening, something they can barely grasp and don't have a name for. Our moment was lifted from the movie *Casablanca*, a movie we both liked to see from time to time: the closing scene when Bogey and Claude Rains slowly walk into the fog that covers the airport.

Suddenly we were jolted by a piercing scream. The woman's kid had thrown his ball at a man in a deck chair a few yards away. The man, dressed in khaki pants and a short-sleeved shirt, was quietly watching children splash around in the water. He had a sweet smile on his face, the kind of smile only a man who's never known the joys of fatherhood can have. But that smile belonged to the past now: the kid's ball had knocked the man's wig off his head, and his face was red with rage. He held his grayish hairpiece in his left hand, and his right was gripping the boy by the arm; people were shrieking with laughter.

"Where's your father?" the man yelled.

"I won't tell you," the kid said. I could see from his expression, even though his arm must have hurt terribly, that he was trying to be brave.

"Oh, yes, you will!"

"I won't!"

"You won't?"

"No!"

When the man placed the kid across his knees to give him a good spanking, I stood up and went over.

"Let him go," I said. "Stop molesting that child. Shame on you!"

"Is this your kid?"

"Let him go!" I said, pulling the kid out of the man's clutches.

"You should teach him better manners."

"Why? He's not my kid. Just like that hair isn't yours. You should be ashamed."

"He's not your kid?"

"I don't think so," I said. "I've always wanted daughters only. Like King Lear."

Something awful bit my hand; when I looked down I saw it was the kid. He met my gaze. Standing with his feet wide apart he was getting ready to slug me. "Bug off, you sad creep!" he said to me. "I can take care of myself!"

"See?" the wigless man said and nodded with satisfaction. "The way Americans bring up their kids!"

"Keep your cool, sonny," I said to the kid. My hand was on fire. "Take your ball and go play somewhere else."

The kid had a crew cut; if he hadn't, his hair would have stood on end from sheer anger. "Next time mind your own bloody business," he told me.

"Okay."

He was still looking at me, and I had the impression he was trying to judge his chances of knocking me down. He couldn't decide whether to kick me in the shins or butt me in the belly with his head, a blow Poles call "the ram." "I bet my daddy could kill you," he said at last.

"Maybe."

"My dad is awfully strong, you know? Once he beat the hell out of two sailors in Naples. Under a bridge, or maybe in a tunnel. Is that your dog?"

"Yes," I said.

"What's it called?"

"Spot."

"Like in that story by London?"

"Yes."

"Okay," he said, shaking his fist at me. "Next time remember to mind your own business." He went off carrying his ball.

"Insolent little brat," the bald man said, still holding his hairpiece in his hand. "I should have given him a good thrashing."

"Better thrash your wig," I said. "If I were you, I wouldn't be caught dead wearing something like that. It makes you less attractive to women. I've read that skin-heads make better lovers. They have more room in their skulls for their hormones."

I went back to my chair.

"Thank you," the woman said.

"Not at all."

"Do you like children?"

"No," I said. "Though I like your kid. I admire his spunk. My sister's got a boy just like that."

"It's hard to bring up a boy when you're alone," she said, getting up, collecting her things.

"Are you going already?" I asked.

"It's almost six," she said.

I got up and took the bag from her hand. "I'm sorry I was so rude. I shouldn't have shouted."

Looking at her face, I thought three or four years from now no head would turn when she walked down the street or went into a movie theater. It's odd how women's looks suddenly disappear and the women themselves, too, vanish without a trace at the age when men become truly handsome and mature. Women's faces grow cold and gray, and they begin to speak in sharp high voices that have no love, no despair, only a kind of miserable wisdom that prevents them from doing reckless things.

"It's okay, really," she said. I gave her back the bag and she smiled at me. "I'm sorry you're having problems."

"Not anymore," I answered. "Not since I made up my mind to go."

She left and I went back to Robert. His skin had taken on a reddish tint, but I knew tomorrow it would be pale as ever.

"What did you tell her?"

"Don't worry. Did I do it right before?"

"You sure did."

"I feel sorry for the dog," I said.

"Don't think about it."

"And I feel sorry for her, too. I feel sorry for them all. Tell the dog to leave me alone."

"Leave him alone," Robert told the dog. The dog went away.

"I feel sorry for all of them," I said again. "They have just one more summer. That's when they try for the last time, with all the money they've been saving for God knows how many years. Then they disappear and are no longer around. I don't mean they leave or go away. They just vanish. And nobody gives a damn. As if they never existed."

"If that mood ever strikes you while you're with her, remember to keep your mouth shut. Otherwise you could ruin everything."

"Don't worry."

"Sometimes I don't know what to expect from you next."

"Robert," I said, "if I had a woman of my own, would I have to talk to her, too?"

"You'd think of something to say."

"No, I wouldn't. The only thing I'd tell her would be: 'Please, I beg you, don't ever talk to me. Don't say a word until the day you decide to leave me.'"

"Not bad, not bad at all. One can tell you're talking from personal experience. But you should speak a little more slowly. I have to keep reminding you of that. Okay, let's go to eat."

"Did I do all right?"

"You sure did. You're great. I told you that long ago, you just don't have enough faith in yourself."

"It's because of the dog," I said. "I can't look at it. I wish everything was over."

"It almost is," he said. "I can feel the money in my pocket. But I just thought of something. You've got to shout."

"When?"

"When you refuse to go away with her. Do you see why? People who know they're wrong always shout. They want to drown out their thoughts with noise. When a man knows he's wrong and is acting against his own convictions, he starts shouting. Don't forget this. It's very important. A simple psychological trick, but it works. You won't forget?"

"No," I said. "I won't."

WHEN WE RETURNED TO THE HOTEL, ROBERT WENT TO SLEEP. I walked out on the balcony. I wasn't hungry and I didn't feel like reading; I stood leaning out and looking at the sea. It was dark and quiet. Our hotel was situated a distance from the city, no noises reached us; I could hear the waves come in and die on the hot sand. It's strange how quickly you get used to hearing the sea and how much you begin to depend on it. It would be unbearable, I thought, to go away and never see the sea again. Motionless, I listened to the purring of the waves and watched the lights blink in the distance. I wasn't thinking of the woman or our dog or what I soon would have to do; the sea released me from all thought and feeling, the way alcohol releases other people. It took me a long time to discover the sea had that power, but it was something I found out for myself so it meant a lot to me. How many things are there, I wondered, that a man can discover about himself without anyone's help? Not many; all that shouting Robert talks about drowns out the way we really are and all the gifts we possess, even though we don't possess so many. So it's a good thing we have at least the sea to look at and listen to. No wise-ass bastard can change that, or try to; that's what felt so good about looking at the sea.

"Aren't you sleepy?" Robert asked.

"No," I answered. "I'm in a philosophical mood. But you go back to sleep."

"I'm trying to, but I can't."

"Nerves?"

"No," he said. "I was thinking about theater. And then about something else. Then I started thinking about the dog. It's costing us a pretty penny."

"How much did it eat today?"

"Two pounds. And it could easily eat twice as much. The butcher at the kosher delicatessen looked at me like I was crazy when I told him all that meat was for my dog. What did you eat today?"

"Some soup and a steak. I spent only a pound and a half."

"This goddamn beast is costing more than both of us together. Maybe we should get rid of it."

"It's up to you. You're the director. I'm only going through the motions. I don't even know my part well."

"One day you'll be a real actor."

"I wouldn't bet on that," I said. "But have it your way."

"You'd make a good one."

"My voice is lousy."

"What do you mean your eyes are lousy? You've got great eyes! Who the fuck told you they were lousy?"

"Nobody said anything about my eyes. I said my voice was lousy."

"Well, work on it. It's all a matter of training. But you'll never be able to play in a comedy. That's your weak point."

"Do you mean that what I'm doing now isn't comic?"

"Depends on how you look at it."

"Robert, let's get rid of the dog."

"No, the dog's not a prop. It's an actor. I've just realized it. It's an actor. You're playing together. And you need it to play out your anger."

"I can break somebody's head," I said. "Even fight a guy twice my size. But let's forget about the dog."

"No. You've got to do something really mean. Something you'll be ashamed of for the rest of your life."

"The worst part is I have to feel ashamed twice," I said. "Both before and after the act."

"You've got no choice," Robert said. "That's why you're

so tragic. Oedipus plucked his eyes out so he wouldn't have to see the world. Think in similar terms. Good night."

At seven in the morning the bouncer came into our room. We were still in bed.

"Listen," he said, "I need to talk to you."

"What about?" Robert asked.

"The deal. I think I'll ..."

"Okay," Robert said, "but not here. There's a cafe on the next corner. Wait for us there. The broad is staying on the same floor. God forbid she overhears anything. And the coffee they serve here is awful. Go. We'll join you right away."

The bouncer left, throwing our dog a timid glance. We dressed quickly and went out into the hall. I was locking the door when I heard a terrible blast: that kid of hers had fired a blank pistol at Robert's ear.

"Don't be afraid, sucker, it's only a toy," the kid said. "But I sure gave you a scare! You're chicken, you know."

It took Robert a moment to regain the power of speech.

"You're chicken!" the kid yelled, reloading his pistol.

"What's your name, sonny?" Robert asked him sweetly.

"Johnny," the kid said. This time he fired at some old crone. She fell against the wall, white as a sheet. "Like Johnny Guitar.

"A doctor," the crone moaned, gasping for breath. "Get me a doctor, hurry!"

"You'll be all right," Robert told her. "Just take a few deep breaths, show more good will to your fellow man, and everything will be tip-top."

Johnny fired his next shot at a waiter carrying a tray stacked with coffee cups; the loud bang of the shot blended rather nicely with the crash of breaking china.

"You obviously have the wrong approach to children," Robert added, addressing the crone. Then he wiped his brow and turned to me. "He says his name is Johnny, but every time I look at him it seems to me he's one of Charles Addams's characters sprung to life. He's the weird boy who's raising a pet pelican in a bottle."

"He'll end up in an electric chair," I said.

"A worse end than that. His cellmates will strangle him and tear his body to pieces. All of America will sigh in relief. But imagine how much the country will suffer before that happens."

When we entered the cafe, the bouncer was already there, drinking coffee, looking embarrassed.

"Listen," he said when we sat down at his table, "I made up my mind. I want out."

"Oh, you do?" Robert asked. "Would you mind telling us why?"

"I've had a better offer. My brother and I are going to make chicken coops for the kibbutzim. We know some people who run a carpentry shop, and we can go into business together. We used to build cooling towers with them. Great guys."

Robert looked like he was going to split apart. "Chicken coops? Are you crazy or something? I'm busting my gut, so is my partner, her kid shoots at me this morning and I think my heart is going to bleed, and you tell me you want to make chicken coops. Why don't you and your brother hatch eggs instead and convert the chicks to the Eastern Orthodox Church before you slaughter them?"

"I don't know how reliable this deal of yours is," the bouncer said.

"Compared to chicken coops it's a cinch. Don't be a child. We've talked about it, shaken hands on it, so now just leave the rest to us, okay? Trust us. All you have to do is collect your cut when I tell you to. Then you can go ahead and start your chicken farm for all I care."

"I didn't sleep a wink the last two nights," the bouncer complained.

"I believe you. He didn't either. But that's your problem.

Buy yourself some sleeping pills and don't disturb us anymore. We're not magicians. We need time. But hard work
and patience always meet their reward. Didn't they teach
you that in school? Listen, do you know the story of Bruce,
the Irish revolutionary?"

"No."

"Bruce was a resistance fighter in the struggle against
the English. One day he was severely wounded, but he
managed to hide in a cave. He was almost certain he was
going to die when ..."

Suddenly our dog growled and we all turned around.
The man who had asked us to buy him a beer the day before had no intention of leaving us alone today either. I
could see he'd done more heavy drinking last night.

"Buy me a Gold Star and I'll go," he said. "I wouldn't
bother you but I'm dying for a drink."

"Why pick on us?" Robert asked. "Aren't there any rich
Americans left in town?"

"I need a drink," the man said, looking at me. It was
clear he hadn't forgotten me.

"You won't bum one from us," I said. "Stop looking for
trouble. Didn't you get enough yesterday?"

"I'm not talking to you," he said. I don't know why he
hated me so much; he didn't even try to hide his feelings.
Maybe he sensed I felt pity for him, and he couldn't stand
that. "Why don't you shut your trap?" he said to me. "Shut
up!"

"You won't get anything from us," Robert said. "What
a nerve!"

"Gimme the money for a beer."

"No. On your way."

He staggered. I could tell he wanted to slug Robert.
I stepped in between them, needlessly, I guess. He wasn't
strong enough to hurt anyone. When his fist hit my arm,
the blow was as weak as a child's. The man was about forty,
tall, and he'd probably been handsome before he started

boozing.

"You know what happens now, don't you?" I asked.

A couple of waiters grabbed him by the shoulders and dragged him out of the cafe, even though he spit all over them and tried to bite. I didn't watch. One of the waiters was a young guy who probably spent all his free evenings at the movie theater on Ben Yehudah Street where a ticket costs only sixty piastres. Now he had his big moment. I heard his blow connect with the drunk's jaw, then there was quiet.

"Lucky us," Robert said. "You could say we're as popular as a shithouse during an outbreak of typhoid fever. Do you know him?" he asked the bouncer.

"Like I told you, we were in the army together. That's all I know. He doesn't know me anymore."

"Okay, it's all settled. Go home and wait for your cut."

"You won't con me, will you?" the bouncer asked. "I don't even know you guys. You won't con me, will you?"

"No," Robert said. "For the love of God, no. Ever since Abraham Lincoln died, there hasn't been anyone as honest as us." He turned to me. "Imagine, I wanted to create a theater for the likes of him. A total waste! There are no values left. That's why no tragedy is possible today. Do you understand what I mean?"

"No," the bouncer said.

"A hundred years ago Art belonged to the aristocracy and the rich. They knew how to care for it. If an actor like Belmondo had appeared on the stage in Paris or St. Petersburg, the theatrical director would have packed his bags the next day. Today Art belongs to everyone. And that's why it's dead. I'm a reactionary. But reactionaries have no power today and Art no longer exists. There are TV sets, cars, and washers you buy on credit, but there's no Art. And there never will be any. There's only Henry Miller and Sartre. Sartre made the astounding discovery that men's underwear sometimes happens not to be very clean, and for that reason alone Sartre will be immortal. He might even be awarded the Nobel Prize. Have you read today's paper? Do you know if they've given that louse the Nobel Prize yet? They should give him one every week. You know who I'm talking about, don't you? That lousy little shit who read Kierkegaard before he was old enough to understand him. Well? Has he got it yet? Come on, tell me."

"I don't know," the bouncer said. "All I know is the fight between Liston and Clay is scheduled for February. That's all I know, Robert."

"You and your goddamn chicken coops. You ought to read Sartre. That would help you understand your chickens. And I wanted to give you great theater! Shit, you don't deserve a thing! You've spoiled the whole day for me. Read Sartre, do anything you like, but don't bother us when we're working. Yes, go home and read Sartre. Read him two or three times."

"When we met in Tel Aviv, you told me you had a foolproof deal, too. And remember what happened?"

"That wasn't my fault. I told you to go and see G. You went to J."

"J. knew nothing about the deal," the bouncer said.

"Of course he didn't. I told you to see G. All you've ever done isn't worth a shit."

"Not worth a shit, huh?" The bouncer was indignant. "I was the one who introduced you to the bellhop in the hotel. That wasn't worth a shit?"

"Nothing you do is worth a shit," Robert insisted.

"Just make sure everything works out this time," the bouncer said in a threatening tone. "You're not gonna roll me."

They continued wrangling like that for quite a while.

Whenever Robert set up a deal, he was very secretive and never mentioned any names, only the initials J. and G. Everybody knew who J. and G. were, but Robert stuck to his code. That was the way he operated.

"G. still owes me money," the bouncer said.

"Read Sartre."

"J. is a thief, too. They threw him in the slammer, but what good is that to me? Am I supposed to follow him there to get my money or what?"

"Read Sartre," Robert said. "Start on him today. And now leave us alone."

We paid for our coffee and walked down to the beach. She was already there. We rented two deck chairs and went to join her.

"Good morning," she said.

"Did you sleep well?" Robert asked.

"I heard Johnny gave you a scare this morning."

"Nothing of the sort," Robert said. "He's a lovely child. And so lively, too. I was just like him as a boy."

While he talked about Johnny and himself, I watched the kid. He was as busy as a one-man band. First he tied a long string to an old man's chair, and when the old poop was about to sit down, he pulled it out from under him. "The kid's got a healthy sense of humor," Robert said, watching the old man try to get up. Then the kid started making mud balls and slinging them at women who didn't want to get their hair wet while swimming. One throw was good enough to ruin a ten-dollar hairdo; his aim was true, and his hand never wavered. He engaged in this activity for some time. I calculated that the hairdressers at the Dan Hotel would earn at least a hundred fifty bucks extra, not including tips. Then he got bored with this game. Suddenly he vanished, and when he reappeared, he had a whole fistful of clothespins. Later I found out all the hotel laundry done during the night had landed in the sand. Johnny stuck the clothespins behind the waistband of his swimming trunks and went into the water. I wondered what he needed them for, but a little later I could have kicked myself for being so dumb. Johnny'd been blessed by Nature with an inventive mind, and this time he had come up with a truly magnificent idea: he swam up to people who wore masks and with one swift motion cut off their air supply by attaching the clothespins to their snorkels; his helpless victims began to suffocate and then tear the masks off their faces; two men lost their masks and never found them again. One of the kid's victims was a lousy swimmer and a lifeguard had to tow him to shore. Everybody started shouting for the police. People were close to a lynching. The man saved by the lifeguard went into hysterics; a crowd gathered around him, and everybody offered the lifeguard advice. The lifeguard lost his head and hit the man in the jaw. The man went crazy and demanded the lifeguard's name: he meant to press charges.

"You'll pay for this!" the hysteric yelled.

"I had no choice," insisted the lifeguard. "I only did what all life-saving manuals tell you to do if someone has a fit."

"You hit me in the face!"

"You had a fit. I had no choice. That's what they taught me in my life-saving course."

"Excuse me, what did they teach you? What is a lifeguard supposed to do?" a stranger wanted to know. He had a distinguished manner of speaking. "What are you supposed to do?"

"Slap him in the face," the lifeguard said. "Like this."

He slapped the distinguished-sounding stranger in the face, but he must have miscalculated the force of his blow because the man fell to the ground like a bird shot in flight, and he lay there motionless on the sand as the lifeguard leaned over him, shouting, "That's what they told us to do in the course. I can show you my manual. These are scientific methods and that man shouldn't resent what I did."

Nobody understood the lifeguard because he was yelling in Hebrew. Little Johnny decided to give him a hand. "He's right. It was his duty," little Johnny said.

"Duty!" the lifeguard yelled, grasping at this word. "Duty! Duty!"

Finally a cop appeared, took down what had happened, and slowly everyone quieted down.

"Johnny, darling," his mother said when the crowd dispersed and Robert and I managed to free the kid from the lifeguard's clutches, "why don't you read something for a while? You'd like that, wouldn't you?"

"I'll give you a book," Robert said.

"Piss on your book," said little Johnny with true feeling. "I wanna play with your dog."

"Of course, sweetheart," Robert said. "I'm sure the two of you will get on famously." Then he turned to me and added softly. "He's gonna kill our dog. We've gotta start looking for a new one."

"What did you say?" the kid asked, eying him suspiciously.

"That we have to feed the dog."

The kid didn't move. He stood in his characteristic stance: feet spread wide apart, his short cropped head lowered and ready to ram you in the belly. His freckled nose was wrinkled in anger. "I'll tell my dad to break your jaw. He's gonna lick you good. Your doctor is gonna make a hell of a lot of money putting you back together.

"Tell us something more about your daddy," Robert said.

"He's big," Johnny said, stretching his arms to show how tall his dad was and how wide his shoulders were; the man must have been built like Sonny Liston. "My daddy is big and strong. He's not afraid of anybody. He can kick the hell out of anyone he wants. Once three drunken sailors ganged up on him, he nearly killed them."

"Really?" Robert asked.

"Really. My dad is strong. He doesn't pick on people, but if someone picks on him, he just ..." The kid paused and then added, "It's a good thing all these insurance agencies are around."

"He pulverized some sailors in Naples," I explained to Robert. "In Naples, under a bridge."

"No, that was another time," Johnny said. "What I'm telling you about now happened somewhere else. I can't remember what that goddamn town was called."

He whistled at our dog, and the two of them scampered away. Robert went for cigarettes. I was smoking the last one. Suddenly she said, "Give me your cigarette, please."

I gave it to her. She didn't try to hide her tears. She sobbed helplessly, uncontrollably; people who were strolling by stopped and looked at her with stupid smiles, then walked off reluctantly. Two fat-faced creeps with drooping bellies stopped in front of us and started whispering to one another.

"Move along," I said.

"What did you say?" one of them said with surprise.

"I said to beat it." They left and I held my hand out to her. "Come. We'll swim out. No need to advertise your problems."

She got up and, holding hands, we went into the sea. Fifty yards from the shore were the remains of an old unfinished pier. We climbed onto the wet planks and sat down.

"How can I help you?" I asked.

"I'm okay now."

"Is it something to do with the boy's father?"

"Yes."

"Johnny's never met him?"

"No. At least I don't think he can remember him. But he'll meet him any day now."

"Are you sure that's a good idea?"

"No, it's not," she said, "but that's why we came here. Johnny's been begging me for so long I finally gave in. Maybe it would have been best to let him just go on imagining his father the way he has up till now."

"I think I understand. But maybe you worry too much. I had an uncle who was the worst person you can possibly imagine; he drank, he played cards, and one day he gambled away the house we lived in. At the same time he was a wonderful person. I loved him more than I loved my mom. My father died when I was five."

"Illness?"

"No, he was killed. Did you ever hear the expression 'a nation of thinkers and poets'?"

"No."

"That's the way the Germans liked to describe themselves. Modesty is a wonderful trait. Now they build a million Volkswagens a year and don't think of the past. Oh, perhaps they feel sorry. The Germans feel sorry after every war."

"Too bad we haven't got any cigarettes," she said.

"Wait for me here. I'll swim back to shore and bring us some. I'm sure Robert has bought them by now."

"No, please stay with me. I'm afraid those two fatsos will swim out here to have one more look at me."

"They couldn't manage it. They probably have hernias and weak hearts and aren't allowed to exert themselves. Lifting a cigarette to their lips is too much for them. Is the boy's father here?"

"Yes, but he hasn't shown up yet. He was supposed to come yesterday. I wrote to him, but maybe something's happened."

"Look, I don't want to appear nosy. Just tell me what you feel like telling."

"His father was born here," she said. "We met eleven years ago when I visited Israel for the first time. He went back to the States with me, but soon he realized he wasn't able to live away from Israel. He came back here, then he began to miss America. So he returned to the States and started dreaming of Israel. And so it went, on and on. Until one day he left and didn't show up again."

"America must be a difficult country to live in," I said. "Of course, it's no fun being a stranger anywhere."

"Yes," she said. "Maybe it wasn't his fault."

I was sure it wasn't his fault. I, too, felt homesick. I longed to go back to Poland. Nothing makes you so homesick as being short of cash.

"Do you want to swim back?" I asked after a while.

"No," she said. "It's nice sitting here. What was this supposed to be? Some kind of bridge?"

"A pier," I said. "A pier with a bar, music, and other nighttime pleasures. But then the guy who started building it went bankrupt. His partner robbed him blind. His wife left him. One of his kids got bitten by a rabid dog and developed a stammer. The poor guy got drunk, climbed in his car, and hit some woman. She took him to court; her lawyer claimed that after the accident she couldn't have sex with her husband because it caused her pain. The court awarded her a huge compensation so that her husband could afford to sleep with hookers. And the man lost his driver's license. He tried to drown himself, but he was rescued and resuscitated, and because he had no medical insurance, he had to pay for the hospital. He next tried to gas himself, then he slashed his wrists, then he swallowed a bottle of sleeping pills, but they saved him every time. He was certified insane, so his wife easily got a divorce and married some rich bastard. Finally the poor wretch plunged a knife into his heart and died in terrible pain in a hospital for the destitute."

"Good god, how do you know all that?"

"I don't," I said. "But if you close your eyes, you can improve on anybody's life. Though if you don't like this ending, I can make up a different one: he let a monkey jump on his back and can still be seen from time to time in the company of leprous beggars. A true Hollywood ending."

"What does he do? I didn't understand you."

"He got addicted to smoking hashish."

"I see. Have you ever been to the States?"

"No."

"You speak with an American accent. You didn't learn that in school, did you?"

"I didn't learn anything in school. I misbehaved so badly they used to make me stand in a corner with my face to the wall. That was my punishment. You have to admit that under those circumstances I didn't stand a chance of learning anything. Even the gym teacher would throw me out the door."

She smiled.

"That's what I wanted," I said.

"What?"

"To see you smile."

"Oh, I'm feeling much better now. So where did you learn English?"

"I worked in the desert for a land-surveyor. You know, one of those guys who runs around with poles measuring distances and can never get their numbers right. My boss was an American and every day for fourteen hours I listened to him curse. After a while we got used to each other."

"You worked in the desert ..." she began.

"Yes," I said. "But please don't say it must have been romantic. It wasn't romantic at all. Lots of scorpions and things like that. Lots of snakes, too, so we had to wear boots all the time. And in the evening my boss would bore me with stories about his family. His mother-in-law was an angel, his wife was an angel, his father-in-law was another angel. Fortunately they all died. All he had left was me and his memories. His angel of a mother-in-law died of a heart attack, his angel of a wife died in a car crash, and his angel of a father-in-law drank himself to death. They all flew to heaven."

"I'm worried about Johnny," she said.

Suddenly she burst into tears again. I stroked her cheek,

remembering to do it clumsily and roughly. You know: a rough man, but a heart of gold. She leaned her head on my shoulder and continued sobbing. I could see she was making an effort to be brave but couldn't help herself.

"Is it something do with Johnny's father? Something bad?"

"This is going to sound awful, but it would be better for Johnny if his father were dead. Oh, God!"

"God will know what's best for the boy. Don't decide for Him."

"You're right. I'm sorry."

"If you have any problems, maybe I can explain things to Johnny for you. I'll come up with some idea for saving the image of his father for him."

"Will you do that?"

"Of course. I like the boy."

"You like him?"

"Sure I do. At times I feel like tearing him to pieces, but that's got nothing to do with it. I like to watch him."

"He likes you, too. And I know why. You resemble the father he's imagined for himself." She looked at me. "Or maybe that's why he doesn't like you. Do you understand?"

"No."

"Hasn't any woman ever told you you're a very attractive man?" she asked. The tone of her voice wasn't pleasant at all.

"No," I replied. "Never."

"Well, then, the women you've had weren't worth a damn."

I didn't say anything, and, even if I'd wanted, I wouldn't have been able to since she quickly added, "Please don't be angry. I'm a straightforward person. If I like someone, I don't beat around the bush. I take full responsibility for anything I say."

I touched her arm. "Are you sure you allow others the

same rights as yourself?"

"Of course."

"Then listen, I like you, too. I think you're very pretty."

"Oh, oh," she said.

"Oh, oh," I repeated, nodding.

"Really?"

"Really. Otherwise I wouldn't be sitting here with you. No one gives a damn about the tears of an ugly woman. If an ugly woman begins to cry, you tell her she's got beautiful eyes and walk away. Too bad, but that's the way men are. As you probably know. What's your name?"

"Mary. I guess it's Miryam in Hebrew."

"I prefer Mary," I said.

"What's yours?"

"Jacob."

"And in Hebrew?"

"Yakov. But the problem is I'm Catholic."

"Is it tough being a Catholic here?" she asked.

"No. If people like you, you can get along anywhere. And people here take pride in being able to offer work and shelter to someone of a different faith. At least, some of them do. There are some who don't like Catholics, but that's not surprising. Let's go back. I'm dying for a cigarette."

"Okay," she said.

When we reached our spot on the beach, I looked at my watch; it was six o'clock. Robert had gone to the hotel. He'd left me a pack of cigarettes and a note: "Take it easy, don't hurry things. And don't forget about your anger and inner turmoil. Little Johnny let our dog loose in a kosher butcher shop. He ate a lot of meat. Big losses. We have to go to the police station tomorrow. Take your time and remember the German saying, 'Patience brings roses.' I'll wait for you in the hotel. Robert." We both lit up and then went to change. I took off my swimming trunks and placed them next to my clothes outside the shower stalls. When I finished showering, I toweled myself and was about to reach for my pants when a small, quick hand darted out from behind the wall and grabbed them. I didn't have to check to know my swimming trunks and shirt had disappeared, too. Clutching a small towel wrapped around my waist, I leaned over the partition and called out to Mary: "Can you hear me?"

"Yes."

"I'm totally naked. Johnny swiped my clothes."

"Your clothes?"

"Yes," I said. "I have a wet cigarette in my mouth, but that's all I got."

"I'll give him a spanking," she promised.

"Later. Right now can you lend me your bathing suit, please? I've got to get back to the hotel."

"In a lady's bathing suit?"

"I'll say I've developed breasts," I answered cheerfully. "Or that I'm a hermaphrodite. It can be quite funny. I don't care. I just want to put something on."

She tossed me her bathing suit and I squeezed into it hastily. I overheard two men talking about me: one said that in California there were lots of men who were attracted solely to members of their own sex, and the other said he had once been to a men's beauty parlor and it was absolutely disgusting. Looking at me pointedly, they both expressed concern for the future of the American nation, which had so quickly ceased to be a nation of pioneers and had completely degenerated. Then the first one told his friend that if he had read the Bible he wouldn't be so surprised, since such things were already known in Sodom and Gomorrah. As well as ancient Greece. The other man said he felt insulted to be talked to like some kind of ignoramus; they left quarreling.

"Well, Johnny," I said to myself, "I think you have a surprise coming. And I don't think you're gonna like it."

"Hey, have you changed yet?" Mary called out.

"I'll be the prettiest girl on the beach," I yelled, "as cute as Debbie Reynolds."

"Maybe I'd better go look for Johnny."

"Don't bother. It won't do any good. He didn't steal my things in order to let you find them. Anyway, he's probably made them into a sail or something else by now."

"Johnny's a monster," she said when I walked out. "I'll give him a good spanking today. On his last birthday he set the house on fire and we had to call the fire engines. My mother almost had a heart attack." She came up to me and kissed me on the cheek. She did it sweetly and naturally, as if she were my sister. "But don't be angry at him, please." Her eyes filled with tears again. "It's all my fault. I don't know how to bring him up."

"I'm not angry," I said. "I never thought I'd look this good in a lady's swimsuit. The floral design is exquisite. I'm sure Robert will appreciate it, too."

"You're very nice, you know? I like you."

That's how it all began. She was only a step away; I held out my hand. We exchanged one timid kiss, then another. The two guys who had quarreled over Sodom and Gomorrah had apparently made up, and now, watching, they started to discuss an Ingmar Bergman movie in which two sisters display rather excessive feelings for each other.

"Pipe down, gentlemen," I said. "Ingmar Bergman is a pipsqueak. That's what Orson Welles said about him and I trust Welles's judgment. This lady, by the way, is my illegitimate daughter."

"Such things were common practice in ancient Greece," the classicist said, as they moved away.

The other one stopped as if struck by lightning.

"I'm fed up with you and your classical education!" he yelled. "Just because I let you lecture me on the Greeks and the Bible, you think I don't know who screwed me on our last deal?"

"And you gave me a bad check," the other cried, close to tears. "If I pressed charges, you'd be in jail. It's no joke!"

They turned in separate directions and went their own ways.

ROBERT LEFT, TAKING THE DOG WITH HIM. HE WAS SPEND-ing the night at the bouncer's apartment so I would have our room to myself. I sat on the balcony, reading Chekhov. I read him all the time, lugging the heavy volumes wherever I went; they were a present from Robert, who also gave me a lecture on Chekhov's greatness. He was right. There are many great writers, but Chekhov is more than that: he's a friend. It always surprises me how cruel he can be at times. I think he was unaware of his own cruelty; it wasn't something he aimed for, which is why he seems so vicious at times. "His imagination was completely lacking anger," Robert said. He had his own ideas of how to stage Chekhov, and he used to talk about them often and at length. The last time he enlarged on his theories was in the Jaffa jail—his audience was a beggar who used to beat his children with an iron rod. I think the beggar understood the lecture; he broke into tears when Robert recited parts of *The Cherry Orchard*. That happens, too.

Robert was a fanatic when it came to theater. In the slammer he always performed for other inmates. He had fixed rates for his artistic services: one cigarette for the *Macbeth* monologue, which begins, "Tomorrow, and to-morrow, and tomorrow," if delivered in Polish, two if in English. The balcony scene from *Romeo and Juliet* belonged to the cheaper classical repertoire: one smoke for the two of us, since I played Juliet. These were the more expensive pieces. The modern stuff I did alone and for much lower rates. Robert never attempted anything contemporary; he was a priest of High Art. I remember how once he and a smuggler, who in his youth had been a member of an amateur theater company in Cairo, came to blows while playing *Faust* together; or rather how Robert started beating the other guy for overacting his role and being too theatrical. When we finally managed to pull them apart, Robert continued to upbraid him, screaming that while on stage an actor should tie the wings of his soul. I was much more modest than Robert; I usually acted out scenes from movies. My greatest success was impersonating Goofy. Naturally, I had more cigarettes than Robert, so he would smoke mine and bitch about the degeneration of public taste and the stupidity of films.

Robert had come to Israel from Poland. His big wish was to create Art. He found employment in a Tel Aviv theater, but they fired him almost immediately because he quarreled ceaselessly with all the actors, criticizing them for following the Stanislavski method, which he found loathsome; this was rather strange since he admired both Elia Kazan and Lee Strasberg. He made such a nuisance of himself and got on everybody's nerves so much they gladly got rid of him at the first opportunity. He then convinced two con men to start a cabaret show, but the first night they had succeeded in insulting everybody: religious zealots and agnostics, fresh immigrants and native Israelis, the press, the army, and God knows who else. The two con men grabbed a taxi and left Tel Aviv right after the performance, pocketing the night's take and leaving Robert alone to face three trials, including one for not paying for the building they had rented for the show. This was how he ended up in jail. He wrote to his erstwhile partners, begging them to help get him out, but they ignored his pleas. He began counseling other inmates, explaining the niceties of the law to them. I met him soon after, sitting on his cot, fat and grubby, giving legal advice to a blind man.

"Okay, tell me what happened," Robert asked him.

"Well, I kind of felt a hankering," the blind man answered.

"A hankering to screw your own daughter?"

"I just wanted to help her fasten her bra," the blind man explained. "She asked me to."

"How often did that happen?"

"Well, now and again."

"You've got nothing to worry about," Robert told the blind man cheerfully. "All you have to do is tell the judge you didn't see who you were screwing. You're blind, aren't you?"

All the inmates roared with laughter, while the blind man burst into tears. Then Robert met a guy who could make puppets, and so—still in the slammer—they started preparing a puppet show together. When Robert was released, he somehow raised the cash to bail out the puppet-maker. The two of them visited me in the hotel where I was staying and turned my room into their workshop. They even made me help them. We worked on those puppets for three weeks, eating only one meal a day: hummus, which the puppet-maker got at an Arab restaurant a block away. When the puppets were finished, Robert persuaded the owner of a semi truck to drive them around; the truck owner became their new partner. They gave two shows in kibbutzim close to the Syrian border; during the third show, devout Jews overturned the semi, burned all the puppets, then chased Robert and his pals for half a mile, showering curses on their heads and spitting on them. The owner of the semi brought charges against Robert, who got locked up again.

I was in bad shape then, too. I couldn't obtain a work permit, but I managed to land a job on a building site in Bat-Yam, and I worked there for a while. One day I slipped and broke my arm, however; a compound fracture. The doctor who set my arm said I would have to wear a cast for six weeks. I didn't have any money for food, and I was really down. An asthmatic burglar staying in the same hotel lent me money for the rent and food. He was a nice guy, born in one of the Arab countries; spoke French like a born Parisian and was rather proud of it. He hated General De Gaulle; said he looked like a sideshow barker and would ruin France. He used to rage that De Gaulle had never been to the front and had cribbed his book on the need for mechanization of the French army from General Guderian; that he had spent the whole war in London spouting drivel over the radio while he should have been fighting the Germans. The burglar went under the nickname of De Gaulle.

Soon afterward the real De Gaulle put down the paratroopers' rebellion, while the "De Gaulle" I knew was arrested for having robbed the cash register at a kosher co-op. A few days later the cops arrested me: some squealer must have told them De Gaulle had given me money. That's how all three of us found ourselves in the Jaffa tank: De Gaulle, Robert, and me. One day I was about to be taken to the examining magistrate, and a guard wanted to handcuff me.

"Come on," I said. "I don't need those. I'll go quietly without the bracelets."

"It's an order," the guard said.

"Nothing doing," I said. "I don't care."

He tried to grab my hand, but I pushed him away. So he went back to the guardroom and I heard him ask the sergeant what he should do.

"You've got to answer violence with violence," the sergeant told him, though I never learned what violence he meant. They came back and beat me unconscious. As soon as I opened my eyes, Robert said, "I have a great idea."

"You're not the only one," I said. "Every hustler in this jail has a great idea."

"I've figured out what to do with you."

"Yeah? What?"

"Thanks to you, we'll both be rich!"

"Nobody's ever become rich thanks to me except for one Hungarian. I got hit by a car and the insurance was paid to him because his name was similar to mine. I never found him."

"He disappeared into the whirlpool of life," Robert said. "But your money won't bring him luck. He'll slip on a banana peel one day coming down the stairs and become a pathetic invalid. He'll sing on street corners and some day you'll pass by and throw him a penny. He'll recognize you, but you won't recognize him. And then he'll suffer even more."

"Maybe so."

"You held yourself nicely in the fight."

"Then how come I've got these on?" I asked, lifting my hands to show him the handcuffs.

"You kept your head high and proud," he said. "I thought to myself that's how Fabrice del Dongo must have looked on his way to the execution."

"I didn't keep it high very long. As you probably noticed, they mainly kicked me in the ass."

"How can Jews act like that?" a pimp complained in a bitter voice. He was handcuffed to Robert; our conversation was taking place in the back of a police van on our way to the magistrate's office. "Jews, who for so long have been beaten themselves. A man comes here out of idealistic reasons, full of enthusiasm and the best intentions, and before he's even had a chance to look around, the police grab him. And this is the Jewish state we've been waiting for for two thousand years."

"Well?" Robert asked me. "What do you say?"

"What do you want me to do?"

"Only what you've always wanted to do yourself. You've wanted to be an actor, right?"

"How did you guess?"

"That's my business."

"I see," I said. "I'm not supposed to know too much. Just like in the stories of that guy who wrote *Guys and Dolls*. You're Spanish John, right?"

"No. Little Isidore. And that bastard over there," he said, pointing to the cop guarding us, "is really Harry the Horse."

"Better watch it, or you'll get an additional charge for insulting a police officer," the cop said.

"So you've read that book, too?" I asked.

"Sure," the cop said. "I just read how Harry the Horse and Big Butch went to crack a safe, and Big Butch took his one-year-old kid with him because he didn't have anyone to leave him with."

"You want me to act?" I asked Robert.

"Yes, but for a very limited audience."

"Who'll pay me?"

"Don't worry. Everything'll be paid for. Leave it all to me; money'll be no problem. You don't mind being paid in American dollars, do you?"

"No, not at all."

Soon afterward De Gaulle was transferred to the Akko penitentiary, where he was to serve out a long sentence, while Robert and I gave our first performance. Everything went just fine; our first client was the American girl who ended up in a nuthouse. That was over a year ago; I remembered it now as I leaned over the balcony rail. The sea in the distance looked misty and dead. I could tell the goddamn wind was coming and that it wouldn't leave the city in peace. It was half past ten; I knew I wouldn't be alone much longer. Thinking of the wind, which would be on us tomorrow, I didn't feel like reading anymore; I didn't even feel like going into the room. I thought of minor, unimportant things; my mind was in a total shambles and I couldn't concentrate on anything. All of a sudden I remembered the day Stalin died. Then I thought of the day Patterson beat Johansson, and of winning a bet from some guy who never paid up; then I recalled how a certain rich but tight-fisted man hired me as a driving instructor for his wife, though he knew I didn't have a teaching permit and that he wouldn't collect any insurance if his wife wrecked the car.

"Can you drive?" he asked me the first day after treating me to a glass of warm soda water with no fizz in it.

"Yes."

"Do you drive well?"

"Yes."

"What sort of make did you drive last?"

"A Wright."

"What's that?"

"A diesel truck. Fifteen tons. Five gears and a reducer."

"Have you had any accidents?"

"One."

His face was shining with sweat; he was worried about his goddamn car—an old Chevy—but at the same time he was too cheap to part with a few pounds more and hire a professional instructor. I watched him, the half-full glass of warm soda water in my hand, while he trembled and sweated.

"Will you be careful?"

"That's something women usually ask," I said. "Sure I will."

"You look as if you enjoyed risky driving."

"I just look that way."

"Do you really drive well?"

"I drove you around a bit, so you should know."

"It's hard to tell after one ride."

"I can drive you around again."

"It'd be a waste of gas," he said. "It's just as hard to tell after two rides. It's hard to tell anything these days. My partner was the best man there ever was, then he started gambling and didn't stop until he gambled away everything. God, I lost a fortune because of him. You just can't tell anything these days."

So I started teaching his wife and she was making good progress, but whenever I came to pick her up for her lesson, I could see she'd been crying. Finally, she told me her husband suspected she was having an affair with me and would kick up terrible fights and come close to a heart attack. Neither of us was attracted to the other. Whenever I made a suggestion, she'd say, "Don't teach me what to do," even though that was exactly what I was paid for. Or, rather, was supposed to be paid for. Each time I came to collect my fee, her husband would pretend he had no small bills; if I reminded him the next day, he would shout at me not to bother him with such trifles since he had a bad heart—so bad, in fact, that the doctors had stopped hiding it from him. He continued to treat his wife so dreadfully that finally one day she and I overcame our mutual repugnance. After that I never went back to their home. I couldn't bear the thought of seeing her again. She kept gobbling sweets all the time, even when she was behind the wheel; she would break a chocolate bar in half and with a heavy sigh push both pieces into her mouth. After that her husband hired a highly recommended professional instructor. The instructor wrecked the car, and both he and the man's wife ended up in the same hospital. Dark forces had conspired against the husband, Robert said.

It was eleven. When the khamsin blows, you close all doors and windows, but I opened the balcony door to go back into the room. At exactly the same moment I opened the balcony door, she opened the door to my room. We stopped and looked at each other.

"Close the door," I said. "That goddamn wind has started."

"I couldn't sleep," she said. "I knocked, but you didn't hear me. So I thought you must be sitting out on the balcony."

"You won't be able to sleep now anyway. When the khamsin comes, nobody sleeps much."

"Where's Robert?"

"He's not here tonight."

"I see." She liked to smile, something I liked about her. "His aging mother cabled him she's not feeling well?"

"No. I told him to get the hell out because I was waiting for you.

"So I didn't surprise you?"

"No. I hate surprises. I fear them more than anything. The only thing that brings joy is something you want and have been waiting for."

"Quite a philosophy."

"No. I just knew we both wanted the same thing."

"That's nice. Listen, you could also say there isn't much happiness in the world, so you shouldn't hesitate doing something you feel some good might come from."

"You took the words right out of my mouth. All I can do is say them again."

"Listen, why do I like you so much? Maybe you can explain that to me."

"No. But that explains why you came."

"Shouldn't I slam the door and leave?"

"We'd lose one night," I said. "And I have just enough money to stay here a few more days. Then I'll have to move. By the way, did you give Johnny a spanking?"

"Yes. He traded your pants for a jackknife with a corkscrew. Johnny says it's a very good jackknife. I brought it with me. I thought you should have it."

She gave me the jackknife.

"Thank you," I said. "Actually I've always wanted one. What about my shirt?"

"He traded it for some kind of lizard."

"Maybe it'll become friends with my dog."

"No. It was a stuffed lizard. Next Johnny traded it for a pack of cigarettes. I brought you those, too."

The cigarettes were Russian; thick as a finger, with cardboard filters.

"I haven't smoked one of these in years," I said. "Only Johnny could have come by them here."

"I'm glad you think so highly of my son."

"Want to try one?"

"Sure. Then what?"

"Let's smoke first," I said. "It'll soothe my nerves."

"Actually it's me who should be tense, not you."

"Not at all. It's me who's afraid."

"Afraid of what?"

"Disappointing you," I said. "And you can't imagine how afraid. I'm not eighteen. This country and this climate have taken their toll."

"Listen," she said. She liked that word. "Listen, I can go if you want. It's just my luck that in this country, where everybody is so goddamn virile, I should be attracted to you."

"Please stay. Maybe I'll muster the courage. Good cigarettes, aren't they?"

"I never knew plain tar could taste this good."

"Yes," I said. "The Russians have lots of good things. In Poland they never stopped telling us how good their scientists were."

"What will we do when we finish smoking?"

"I'll tell you something about my childhood. I once had a friend who experimented on frogs. The frogs really hated that. That was in Poland."

I fell silent.

"Is that your only memory from Poland?" she asked after a terribly long pause, when she must have lost all hope of my continuing the conversation.

"Actually the only thing I really remember from Poland is Khrushchev's face," I said.

"You're a very strange lover."

"I know. Once for three nights in a row I explained the construction of a steam engine to some girl. It didn't get me very far. But apparently I was very cheeky as a kid. You'll have to excuse me for a moment. This room doesn't have a toilet."

"Okay," she said.

I went out into the corridor. There was a buzz in my ears and a total void in my mind. I went down to the reception desk and called Robert from there. When I heard his voice, brisk and eager, I felt a little better.

"Bobby, quick," I said. "I've forgotten how it goes after the initial nonsense. It's because of the khamsin. Why don't we wait a few days?"

"Are you crazy? Think how much we're paying for that goddamn hotel room. We can't wait, damn you."

"Then what am I supposed to do now?"

"Don't touch her yet. Tell her what you're going to do to her, but keep away. Wait until she gets so hot she can't stand it."

"What if she doesn't get hot?"

"She will. No woman can resist for long if you tell her what you intend to do to her. Even St. Therese of the Child Jesus would have given in. Can't I ever leave you alone? You're like a child, you know?"

"Okay," I said, putting down the receiver. I went to the hotel bar and drank a beer and listened to two German Jews talk about Goethe.

"He was a great man," one of them said.

"What do you mean great? He was the greatest!"

"And so cheerful," the first one gushed.

"He was our greatest poet," the second one said.

They were both corpulent and elegantly dressed; I was certain they had spent the war in Switzerland or in the States. I looked at my thin face and bleached hair in the mirror over the bar, gulped down the rest of my beer, and turned to them: "Das beste, was Goethe geschrieben hat, ist *An American in Paris*, meine Herren."

I bowed and went upstairs. She was standing by the closed window, taking deep breaths. Her forehead was covered with sweat, but that didn't make her any less attractive. Or maybe she wasn't perspiring. Maybe it was only my imagination.

"It's all because of this wind," I said. "I'll tell you what happened once in Haifa, when after four days of khamsin ..."

"I think it's time you shut up," she said.

"No. I'll decide what comes when. Nothing I desire will pass me by, but I want it to last a long, long time. So that I'll never forget. First I want to think about it, then talk about it, and only then do it."

"You haven't said anything yet."

"But I'm going to now. I'm thinking you'll be naked soon and that while I'm undressing you, something may rip. I'm thinking that your breasts are small and your legs strong. And I know your belly is flat and hard. And that afterwards we'll lie next to each other smoking the cigarettes Johnny contrived to get us. And I'm sure we'll speak softly to each other, even though we could speak quite loudly because we're all alone. We'll both be a little uncomfortable. I'll feel your hair on my lips."

"Don't say anything more."

"No. I'll go on talking. I'll talk until we both go mad. I'm thinking of your belly, whether it's strong and hasn't been disfigured by Johnny. Maybe it has tiny light scars which I'll be able to feel with my fingertips. I hope so. Maybe I can kiss them once you stop feeling shy. And soon my shyness will also disappear and you, too, will be able to kiss me. And then we'll start again, and the whole room, the bed, everything will have your smell. Not mine, but yours. But until I say that one important word, this is all."

"I have to leave Israel," she said.

"So leave. Go wherever you like, remember me only as long as it brings you joy."

"What if afterwards nothing brings me joy?"

"No man should be so conceited as to believe no other man can replace him."

"Do you believe that?"

"No."

"Neither do I."

"Don't think about it now," I went on. "Think what I've been telling you. Think of me taking off your dress very, very slowly, and other things. Think only of that."

"I love you, you know?" she said. "I'm glad I said it first. I really am. Did you hear me? I said it first. Will you remember that?"

ROBERT SHOWED UP AT THE BEACH AROUND TEN. HE LOOKED dreadful. It turned out the bouncer had only one bed and they had had to share it. What's more, the bouncer's girlfriend dropped in unexpectedly and kicked up a row when she found them in bed together. Somehow they managed to calm her, but then had to share the bed with her, too. The dog slept stretched across their feet.

"The bouncer's worried about his money," Robert said. "He kept me awake half the night talking about it."

"He'll get his cut," I said.

"I've got a new bride for you."

"Oh, yeah?"

"We'll have to start on her as soon as we finish with this one. She's arriving from the States on the fifteenth and going straight to Tiberias. A bellhop I know told me."

"But you had to phone him, didn't you?"

"What's the difference? As soon as we finish with this one, we'll go to Tiberias."

"No," I said. "It's too hot over there this time of year. Around 120° in the sun. I'll suffocate."

"You'll be okay. I hear she's a very nice girl. We have to start looking for a new dog. There's a bulldog I'd like, but the owner wants eighty pounds. That's too much."

"You won't get a purebred for less."

"I'll try."

"Spot cost us a hell of a lot of money, too."

"But just think what a dog he is," he said. "Like a forest fire or a typhoon."

I glanced at Spot; little Johnny was chasing him.

"I can't think about him," I said. "Every time I see him,

I begin to feel dizzy. The dog we had before was nothing compared to this one."

"Yes, Spot is an exceptionally lovable beast. But it can't be helped."

"Let's leave out that part."

"No, that's impossible. We might just as well pack our bags and get the hell out of here. Remember, I'm the one responsible for the whole deal. Don't worry. You'll have plenty of rest when we get to the Sea of Galilee. Everything will be fine. Just think: you, your despair, the woman you love, the lake Jesus walked across ... Listen, that's not work, that's pleasure. You can quote from the New Testament to her. Maybe some passage from St. Paul's First Epistle to the Corinthians, the one on love and charity. A historical spot, love, Arabs shooting at night, your despair, a tornado of sensuality; it should be child's play."

"Oh, shut up," I said. "Even here it's too hot to breathe. I don't want to think of Tiberias."

"Take it easy. You don't know how to enjoy yourself. How are things going? Okay?"

"Yes."

"See? I told you."

"You were right," I said. "You proved to me what human genius is capable of."

"Good. I'll go talk to the bouncer now and try to convince him to back us again. Though I'm afraid he'll be reluctant to risk any more money."

"We don't need him. When we pull off this job, we should have enough money for Tiberias."

"I don't think it's a good idea for us to finance ourselves. I'm sure everything'll work out fine, but what if it doesn't? It's always better if somebody else takes the fall. The same as with a movie production."

"Only no one will give us an Oscar, no matter how good we are," I said. "And that's the bitter truth."

"You're an actor, not a star. Remember that. Anyway,

Chaplin didn't get an Oscar either."

"But he got American dollars in Swiss bank accounts. And all he has to pay is four percent income tax."

"God willing, one day you'll be wallowing in money, too. Okay, I'm going. Think of the Sea of Galilee. You'll have to be in the depths of despair. These broads go for that. Despair above all. Think about it."

"It's enough if you do," I said.

Robert left. Soon afterward I heard a piercing scream, which must have reached the highest heavens. Little Johnny's sense of humor had led him too far this time: when some lady swam out to sea on an inflatable rubber mattress, he punctured it with his knife, letting all the air escape; the mattress sank almost immediately. I could see the lifeguard holding Johnny under his arm and a crowd trying to resuscitate the poor woman. The lifeguard began walking in my direction, as unrelenting as fate.

"Is this your kid?" he asked, trembling with anger.

"It's awfully hot," I said. "Ask me a simpler question."

"Do you know what I'm going to do now?"

"I have no idea."

"I'm going to whack his ass so hard he'll have to crawl on his belly for a week. Everybody's had enough of him!"

"He's a good kid," I said. "Let him go, or the blood will rush to his poor little head."

"Are you responsible for him?"

"Yes."

"Are you absolutely sure?"

"That's right."

He let go of little Johnny, who then managed to bite his captor somewhere near the liver. The lifeguard threw down his fancy hat with a brass anchor, the word **lifeguard** stitched on it.

"I'm talking to you as a private person now," he said to me. "Get up from that deck chair."

"It's too hot," I said. "Come back when the khamsin

stops blowing."

"Be a man!"

The tone of his voice was so imploring, I had to oblige. He hit me in the jaw with such force I fell back on the chair, breaking it to pieces. Then he lost his balance and tumbled down; I grabbed him by the hair and kicked him in the belly. He gasped, but managed to hit me once more. I, too, managed to land a blow with the last of my strength. Then we both sat on the sand, breathing hard.

"I'm afraid we won't be able to continue," I said. "I'm out of breath. It's because of this goddamn wind."

"You're right," he said. "I feel kind of weak myself today. What I need is a cup of strong coffee."

"Your legwork is lousy. That's why you lost your balance."

"And you don't know how to kick. You were aiming at my gut, but you got me in the groin."

"Too bad I don't know karate," I said. "If I did, I could kill you by hitting your Adam's apple with the edge of my hand."

"Sure. If I let you," he said, rubbing his belly. "But I could dodge your blow and then hit you right between the eyes. The nasal bone would break and knife into your brain. Instant death."

"Karate is a clever art."

"But you have to learn it well. Another good move is to hit someone in the solar plexus with the tips of your fingers. But you have to be careful not to break your fingers. It's best to wrap a hanky around your hand. Real tight."

We fell silent. We were both breathing hard; the lifeguard massaged his belly, I massaged my jaw.

"I lost my job because of this kid," he said. "I just couldn't take it anymore. I've been following him around for the past three days, but there's no way to keep him out of mischief. Yesterday he managed to get hold of a magnifying glass and set fire to guests' pockets, the pockets they kept their money in, of course. As I was carrying him just now, I got so angry something snapped in me. I lost my job, but I don't give a damn."

"You'll find a new one," I said.

"Small chance. The season's almost over. All the hotels already have lifeguards. I won't find anything."

"You should go to Eilat," I said.

"What for?"

"I know some guys down there. They could find you a job in Solomon's mine. Or in the harbor."

"I prefer the harbor."

"It can be arranged."

"I'm willing to give it a try," he said. "And you don't have to pay taxes in Eilat. Can you really help me?"

"Sure. When you get there, ask for Abram Szafir. He's a wonderful guy. I stayed with him two years ago. He'll help you find something. Can you play cards?"

"Of course."

"Then don't have second thoughts about going. A good player is worth his weight in gold there. Everybody's bored stiff; playing cards is the only entertainment."

"Will you write me a note to your friend?"

I wrote a note and gave it to him. The lifeguard picked up his fancy hat and handed it to me.

"Give it to the kid. Actually, I never wanted to be a lifeguard."

He left. I got up, too, and started searching for Johnny. When I found him, he was busy building a fortress on an old gentleman in the sand. The old man was watching him with a kindly expression.

"You should buy him a toy," the old man said. "Maybe a spear gun, something like that."

"You don't know him," I said. "The only toy he'd enjoy playing with is a flamethrower. Come, Johnny. Come along, dear. There's something we have to talk about."

He stood up and followed me.

"Yesterday you traded away my pants and my shirt," I said. "Then you let our dog into a meat store and the poor animal ate so much it hasn't been able to eat since. The chair the lifeguard broke throwing me onto'll cost at least thirty pounds. I just want you to know the holy saints don't shower money on me from the sky, and I don't expect them to start anytime in the near future." I gripped his shoulder and turned him toward me. "The fact is I'm a poor man, John. I'm sorry to have to tell you that."

"You mean you don't have money?"

"No, John. I never had any."

"Try making some."

"That's excellent advice, John. But it so happens I haven't got any money now."

He held out his hand. "I'm sorry."

"That's okay," I said.

"Listen, do you want to sell your dog?"

"No, Johnny. Spot isn't for sale."

"I'd like to have it," he said. "It's a good dog. And Americans love dogs."

"Yes, I know. Americans love dogs more than any other nation does. But Spot isn't for sale."

"Spot would like it in America."

"I know, John. But I can't sell you my dog. It's too late now, and it can't be changed."

"Too late?"

"Maybe I've expressed myself wrong. But Spot has to stay with me and that's it. Spot is my only friend."

"How about Robert?"

"Listen, John. Spot isn't going anywhere. Period."

"There is a way out," Johnny said. "I think I know how to get that dog to the States."

"What do you mean?"

"Can I talk to you man to man?"

"You can try."

"It seems that my mom loves you, you know?"

"I know," I said.

"Do you love her, too?"

"Yes, I do, John."

"Listen," he said, "did either of you think what is gonna happen when my daddy finds out? He's gonna kick the shit out of you!"

"I'll have to defend myself. That's all I can do."

He looked at me with a crooked smile. "Man, you don't stand a chance!"

"Even if I don't, I'll still have to fight. Wouldn't you?"

"Sure I would. But I feel sorry for you. I know my daddy. Look, have you kissed my mom?"

"Yes, I have."

"And she kissed you?"

"She's kissed me, too."

"Then it looks real bad for you. Listen, just don't tell my daddy that. I know it's not right, but I worry for you all the same. If my daddy finds out, he's gonna kill you. As things stand, he might do it anyway. Listen, did I ever tell you about the time some bums picked a fight with him in a bar on Russian Hill in San Francisco?"

"No."

"Actually there isn't much to tell. When he was done with them, they were barely breathing. Anyway, remember what I just told you."

"Okay. I will."

He turned to leave, then stopped. "Actually, you're okay, you know? You weren't bad in that fight with the lifeguard. You're quick."

He walked away, taking the dog with him. All in all, a lovable kid. Then I groaned softly; the lifeguard had landed a few good ones. I felt so lousy I decided to get drunk that evening. I thought the thief crucified next to Jesus must have been meek as a lamb compared to little Johnny. No doubt about it. And then, after a while, I began to think of Johnny's father, and that made me feel even worse.

But I didn't get drunk in the evening. I lay in bed with her head resting on my shoulder as we watched the sea, motionless and silent, through the open balcony door. The moon seemed glued to a sky suffocating under a heavy fog; the world looked empty and dark.

"When this goddamn wind stops blowing, he'll start talking again," I said.

"Who? You mean the sea?"

"Yes"

"Why do you think of the sea as masculine? English grammar is of a different opinion."

"I don't give a damn. I just wish he'd start talking again. That's all."

"California is by the sea, too," she said softly.

"Don't."

"Wouldn't you like to go there?"

"No."

"Every time I look at you and Johnny ..."

"Then stop looking at us. I'm not going to California."

"But you want to go to Australia."

"I have a job there."

"Listen, you think there aren't jobs in America? Don't be ridiculous."

"I'm too old for America. It scares me. I love America too much to risk disappointment. It probably seems strange to you, but that's the way I feel. I'm a Pole. All Poles are cripples. America doesn't need cripples."

"Why do you call yourself that?"

"Because it's true," I said. "And it can't be changed. I wanted to be an actor once, but it didn't work out. I didn't finish high school, so the Actors' Studio rejected me. I could have tried again some years later, but my nerves gave out. I started writing, but that didn't get me very far, either, goddamn it. Then I came here, because I wanted to see the place immortalized in the Bible. I don't have a work permit, so I have to report to the police every two weeks and explain how I manage to survive. But soon it'll all be over."

"Calm down. Take it easy. It's all because of this wind. It's making everybody crazy. You'll come with me."

"I never said that."

"You will, tomorrow."

"Listen," I said. I, too, had started saying "listen." She and Johnny had taught me that. "Listen, it's not only that. I'm a loser. And I'd keep on losing on the other side of the ocean. I like clear situations. For me, Australia is the end of the road, and I know it. In America it would take me more time to free myself from new illusions."

"I don't care about America or Australia. I care about us."

"There's nothing we can do," I said. "Listen, when you're twenty years old, you despise compromises. Later, you begin to accept them because there isn't any other way. Then one day you learn to feel happy just because the woman you love is alive somewhere. And who she is with ceases to be important. You're happy because she's alive and breathing." I paused a long time, then added, "And that's the onset of old age, which comes too soon."

"Have you had so much love in your life you can reject this love?"

"I'm not rejecting it. Like I said, it'll be with me the rest of my days. As a beautiful memory to be cherished forever. Something that has nothing to do with the goddamn rat race of having to explain to everybody why after so many years I still don't have a secure job."

"I don't have much," she said. "But my father did leave some money when he died. Why don't you take it and do something with it?"

"I don't know what to do with money."

"Look, we'll find some way of investing it. Let's just try to be happy as long as we can."

"That's not possible," I said. My jaw still ached from

the lifeguard's blows. There was a buzz in my head and I couldn't concentrate. I didn't remember what I was supposed to say to her next, and I didn't feel like going down to the lobby and phoning Robert. I remembered seeing a huge gorilla of a man that morning lying on the beach watching little Johnny. I imagined Johnny playing some prank and the gorilla losing his temper and going after me. I shuddered. I heard my rasping breath in the darkness; I got up, turned on the light, and approached the mirror. I leaned my forehead against the glass but got no relief; the mirror was warm and slippery.

"Go to your room," I said.

"I won't leave you alone now."

"Go away, I want to sleep. This is all so incredibly stupid, and the wind is getting on my nerves. Go to hell. I don't want you or the money your father left you. I moved into this hotel to con you out of some dough; Robert was going to help me. Some other things were to happen, too, but I'm glad it's all over now." I turned away from the mirror and closed my eyes, but the instant I did that, I saw the gorilla coming at me, his jaw clenched in fury. I opened my eyes and met her stare; the expression on her face was both amused and watchful. "I hustled other women before," I said. "But right now I've had enough. Not that I've become more sensitive all of a sudden, or that I want to reform. I'd be happy to live this way for a thousand years. But I don't feel too well today. I'll be going to Tiberias next, together with Robert, where we'll try to swindle some other girl. I have no plans to leave for Australia. I don't even know where it is."

She laughed. "Why don't you tell me you have a wife and kid, and that's why you need money?"

"I don't have any kids. I've spent more money on abortions than there is in the Vatican budget. Even though I'm careful. As you've probably noticed." I went over and sat on the bed.

"Easy," she said. "Easy. It'll pass. It's all because of this wind. Don't talk. There's no need to talk. I'm here with you."

She put her arms so tightly around me I couldn't move. The silence was total: I could hear the slow, painful beating of my heart and her quiet whispering. This is probably how she had spoken to Johnny when he was very small and had trouble falling asleep. I think God created her so that she would give men love, peace, and rest. So that she could make them tired and then make them sleep. I'm sure He forgave her everything.

"I'm just a cheap gigolo," I said. "It's not my fault if you don't want to believe me."

"You're a big boy who probably started shaving too soon," she said. "In America you'll buy yourself a sports car and wreck it. I'll help you do it. Now go to sleep. Sleep in peace. It's all because of this wind."

I didn't answer. I didn't know what to say; I had spoken my own lines, departed from Robert's script. I didn't know how to continue. Robert would have been able to advise me, but he wasn't there. Lying next to her, I tried to imagine her face in the darkness. It was very pleasant to lie like that, totally still, and imagine her face, her good and pretty face, which I would have been able to see if I turned on the light. But I didn't turn it on; I lay next to her, motionless, thinking of her face; then I thought of her soft sloping belly and the small, light scars she had from giving birth to Johnny. She smelled the way a woman should, with a smell resembling the aroma of ripe corn, gentle and strong. There was nothing it could be compared to; and now the bed and this small, dark room were permeated with it. I moved my hand slowly down her flat, warm belly; she clasped my hand between her thighs and now, with the sheet thrown back, her aroma became more intense. When she leaves this room in the morning, I thought, her smell will disappear after a time, though it would be so much nicer if this room and this city retained her smell forever; then I would always remember she was with me once and life would somehow be more bearable; maybe I would think about her in Tiberias, my next destination, or even years from now, lying in bed with some other woman.

I should have told her all this. I wouldn't have needed Robert and his goddamn instructions to do it either. There was so much I could have told her about myself and my life, but she probably wouldn't have believed me. I could have told her how I robbed someone when I was fifteen and wasn't caught. And how three months later a friend and I robbed a ticket office at a train station; my friend was arrested, and I gave myself up so we could go to jail together, because I enjoyed his company. But she wouldn't have believed me. Nor would she believe me if I told her I lost my virginity at the age of twelve to a ripe German girl on the day of her engagement to a young lieutenant. Nor would she believe me if I told her about the German soldier who set his dog on me and then started kicking me and broke my nose just because I wanted to play with the dog—this happened when I was seven. Nor would she believe me that in 1944, in Warsaw, I saw six Ukrainians rape a girl from our building and then gouge her eyes with a teaspoon, and they laughed and joked doing it. Maybe I myself didn't believe all this anymore. I should have told her that I bear the Germans no grudges for killing my family and a few more million Poles, because afterward I lived under the Communists and came to realize that by subjecting men to hunger, fear, and terror, one can force them to do anything under the sun, and that no group of people is better than any other. Those who claim otherwise belong to the lowest human species and their right to live should be revoked.

I should have told her: Listen, I'm just a fucking Polack, and I should have told her my life hadn't prepared me for any other way of living, that none of my experiences would ever come in handy, just as I myself was of no use to anyone, unable to offer any good or any worthwhile advice, because no one would ever believe me if I tried to. And that's the truth. But I didn't say these things. I lay next to her and the warmth of her body enveloped me and put me to sleep, and there was nothing else I wanted to feel or think about.

It would have been a relief to tell her everything. It would have been a relief just to tell her about the Jewish family hiding next door until they were murdered by the Germans. A man, a woman, and three children: when their bodies were lying on the ground, the Germans stopped some men walking by and ordered them to piss on the corpses; a German called me over and I pissed, too, shaking with fear, while the Germans photographed the living profaning the dead. And it would have been a relief to tell her how one day when I was walking to school, the Germans blocked off the street and made us watch them hang people from balconies; no one moved or screamed, not those forced to watch, nor those who were being hung. But how was I to tell her all that? I didn't know. How could I tell her about the girl who fell in love with a German soldier, and, although she had done no one any harm, one day members of the underground caught her, pushed an empty half-liter vodka bottle up her vagina and broke it; she died a few days later. I could have also told her about the Jewish mothers in 1943 who threw their babies into a raging fire, first lifting them high over their heads as if in a gesture of triumph, while Poles made funny remarks from the other side of the ghetto wall. But I think she would have asked me to shut up after my very first words. I tried to tell these things to lots of people, but I don't think anyone ever listened seriously.

I pulled the sheet off her and turned on the lamp. She slept as calmly and peacefully as a child. Her belly was brown, with a golden thread of hair going up from her pubes. Her legs were a bit on the heavy side, her breasts small; dressed up in lace she would have been the perfect model for somebody forging Renaissance portraits. The minute scars on her belly were almost invisible, and I could barely feel them under my fingertips. Suddenly she opened her eyes and her hands began moving, quietly and slowly, waking my desire. And she asked softly, "You will come with me, won't you?"

"No," I said.

I woke about two hours later. She was no longer in the room. Once again I started to think of the gorilla on the beach and what he would do to me. With the tip of my tongue I could feel the roof of my mouth was swollen. The lifeguard had a forceful punch. Tomorrow I'll really be swollen, I thought; I'll have to go to the dentist and ask him to cut the swelling open. I'll have to sit in his waiting room for at least an hour and listen to all the other patients tell sickening stories of their own dental problems.

Everything seemed frightening and unbearable. The world was a dark, stinking alley, which I would have to wander in forever. I felt as if I'd entered the nightmare of a crazy man or a drunk. I told myself it was all because of the wind, but that didn't help. I had the premonition something tragic was about to happen, but I didn't know where to run or hide.

I put on my clothes and went downstairs. The hotel clerk was sleeping with a newspaper over his face and I had to shake him by the shoulder several times before he woke up.

"How much do we have to pay?" I asked.

"Are you leaving right now, sir?"

"Tomorrow. How much is it?"

"For yourself only, or for both you and the other gentleman?"

"Both of us."

He started checking his books, but couldn't get the right sum right away; he would add something first, then subtract, then add again, but finally he said: "A hundred and thirty pounds. Will you and the other gentleman be staying for breakfast?"

"Yes."

"Then it'll be a hundred and thirty-five."

"Okay."

"Your friend has already paid a hundred pounds. So you only have to pay thirty-five."

No way we can leave the hotel now, I thought. There's too much to lose; since Robert already put down the money we got from the bouncer, we have to go on with the hustle. Otherwise the bouncer will follow us to hell to get the money we owe him.

I looked at my watch: it was one o'clock. I left the hotel and started walking toward the city. I knew what I planned was stupid and senseless, but I went on anyway. At a certain point a cat with its tail held almost straight up began to follow me along the dark streets. I entered the building where Azderbal lived. I knocked, but nobody opened the door. The cat watched me from the darkness with its honey-brown eyes.

I turned the door knob and went in. I crossed to the empty dining room; so did the cat. I went into the bedroom and switched on the light. Azderbal wasn't there; only his girl friend, and she was a heavy sleeper. I sat on the bed next to her, trying to gather my thoughts and decide why I'd come here. Then I remembered the bouncer who'd invested in us, the gorilla waiting for me at the beach, and also Johnny's father, who would probably knock me out with one blow. I looked at the cat who sat devotedly at my feet.

"Come here, Stanislaw," I said to the cat, and it jumped on my lap. The girl woke up and lay there staring at us. "His name is Stanislaw," I told her.

"What do you want?"

"Money," I said. "I intend to sell Stanislaw to you. Where is that he-man of yours?"

"He's gone to Haifa."

"When will he be back?"

"In two days."

"I can't wait that long. You have to give me two hundred and thirty pounds. Once you do, Stanislaw is yours."

"Why did you come to me?"

"Because I'm crazy. And so are you. Who do you think I should have gone to?"

"And if I refuse to buy Stanislaw?"

"You'd better not. Or I'll force you to."

She got up from the bed and went to the mirror. She tidied her hair; watching her I could swear she wanted to make herself look attractive not only for me but for Stanislaw, too.

"Would you like a drink?"

"I wouldn't mind some brandy," I said. "Do you have any in the fridge?"

"Why don't you check?"

I went to the refrigerator and took out a bottle of brandy and a fish for Stanislaw. Then I returned to the bedroom and poured a glass for each of us.

"How much do you need?" she asked me after a moment.

"Two hundred and thirty pounds," I said. "That includes tomorrow's breakfast. I have to pay for my hotel."

"So far you've always moved out without paying the bill and it never bothered you. Once you even left a girl behind and she had to pay. I was that girl, remember?"

"That's not a bad idea. How come I didn't think of it earlier? I'll do what you say."

"You need the money for some woman. There's a woman involved, isn't there?"

"Yes."

"And you don't want to play a dirty trick on her."

"I can't just move out," I said. "Robert already paid for the hotel. And it wasn't our money. We have to pay back what we owe or we'll be in trouble."

"Come off it. You're never in trouble. Even if a hundred women refuse to give you money, you still always find one."

The cat finished eating the fish and meowed. I got up, took out another fish from the fridge, and gave it to him.

"Poor old male whore," she said, staring at me. "Has to go chasing around in the night while everybody else sleeps, and no one will give him any money."

"You will," I said. "Would you like another drink?"

"Yes, please."

We drank some more brandy. I stared at her legs and realized she was still quite pretty.

"Five years ago you must have looked like a fresh flower," I said. "Did you wear white dresses?"

"Yes."

"Do you still have them?"

She went to her wardrobe and took one out.

"Nobody wears long dresses anymore," she said. "They've gone out of fashion."

"Put it on."

She stared at the dress for a moment, then threw it on the bed. She sat down at the table and poured herself half a glass.

"Do you still drink as much?" I asked.

"And you?"

"I can't afford it. Anyway Robert hates alcohol."

"So what do you do with the money you score?"

"Nothing much. We go to the movies. Robert eats a lot. Our expenses run high."

"I only have a hundred pounds," she said. "I'll give it to you."

She took five twenties out of her purse and handed them to me. I put them in my pocket.

"Wait," she said. "I forgot something."

She stretched out her hand and I gave her the bills back. She threw them on the floor, and bent down and spat on them.

"You can take them now. They're all yours."

I leaned over and picked up the bills. When I looked at her, she burst into tears and flung herself on the bed.

"Go away," she said after a while.

So I did.

As I walked back along the empty streets, I could tell the wind had changed direction. The sky over the sea was beginning to pale, which made me feel a little better. I knew the khamsin would stop blowing soon. I was about to turn toward my hotel when suddenly I remembered my friend the hunchback who had trouble sleeping at night, too, and was probably sitting in front of the john in the hotel on Allenby Street. I felt like talking to him, so I climbed up the stairs and tiptoed past Harry, who was sleeping with a detective novel in his hand. I glanced at the cover; it was the one where Mike Hammer shot his girlfriend in the belly with his .45. I had read it in prison. Mickey Spillane's novels weren't allowed in jail, and for that reason they were the most popular books there. I remembered I had to pay three or four cigarettes for reading that one.

The hunchback was sitting in his usual spot.

"I can't sleep," I said.

"You're telling me."

"Do you have any sleeping pills?"

He raised his eyebrows. "You're the one who should have them. Or have you quit your profession?"

I looked at my watch. "Four o'clock. Too late to take any pills. I'd need at least six hours to sleep them off."

"How's business?"

"Fine. How about your priests? Did they give you the money?"

"Yes. Last night. They also gave me a book about missionaries. I'm reading it now. I just found out the most missionaries ever murdered were in China."

"Listen, do you still want a broad? I have an idea."

"What?"

"Come with me. You won't have to pay anything."

He looked doubtful. "You mean it?"

"Sure. We'll play a complicated joke on somebody."

"Wait, I'll just take some charcoal pills. My goddamn stomach ..."

When we arrived at Azderbal's apartment, the lights were already out. The hunchback slipped quickly into her bed, and I left. I woke around eleven, feeling much better. I thought of the girl; she must have had a terrible hangover and a hunchback was just what she needed in 105° heat. Then I decided I wouldn't split the money she gave me with Robert, and my mood improved even more. I'm always sublimely happy when I hit on a scheme to con a partner. Nothing can quite compare with that state of bliss and contentment. I showered and went downstairs for breakfast, bowing to all the ladies I met on the way. I ordered four scrambled eggs. Robert looked sleepy and pale and had big circles under his eyes; sharing a bed with the bouncer wasn't the most comfortable way to spend the night. After breakfast we walked out to the beach. Azderbal's girl friend must have wakened by then and discovered it wasn't me who had returned in the middle of the night to cover her with caresses. God knows what is really funny.

In the afternoon we took the bus to Jaffa. Robert knew a fellow there who had a dog for sale, but somehow we couldn't find him. We went to a cafe we knew he frequented and ordered coffee. The man finally showed up and said he'd get the dog.

"You know something, Robert?" I said after the man left. "Last night I forgot my lines and since you weren't there, I made them up myself."

"What did you tell her?"

"I told her it's all an act, that we're after the money."

"You didn't!" he exclaimed, turning pale.

"I did. But don't worry, she didn't believe me. It came

out beautifully. I'll always do it from now on."

Robert sat motionless, not saying anything.

"You're upset because it was my idea. Come on, Bobby. Admit it. You're jealous."

"You could have ruined everything."

"But I didn't. Why, it only improved my psychological makeup. I'm a complicated and unhappy person, my pride is hurt, interpret it any way you want."

"Did you tell her everything?"

"Enough."

"Did you tell her about the girl from Boston?"

"No."

"You didn't tell her she committed suicide?"

"No."

"You should have told her everything. That first she had to be locked up in a nuthouse and that a year later ..."

"I don't like to talk about it."

"Then don't talk about it at all. Look, I haven't forgotten what kind of person you are. A man at odds with himself, even slightly unbalanced, but the idea that you could take money from a woman should be so abhorrent to you it shouldn't even cross your mind. The way I present you is different and much more modern. Don't forget the times we live in. I show you only in those situations which are essential to your character— when you're in despair, in love, or seething with fury. The rest she can fill in herself. Look how Americans make films. They show only the key situations, the most important ones which move the action forward, and that's why it's all so convincing."

"Then you have to come up with some new lines for me. There's something missing from my performance, Robert. There's a vacuum at one point. I felt this yesterday, and that's why I departed from the script. Just after I refuse her offer to take me to the States—I don't know how to go on."

"At this point you should play a man at peace with him-

self. You've made up your mind. You're like a man con-
demned to death being led to the firing squad, a man fully
in control of his senses who knows this is the end. Understand? Ask her to tell you something about America, ask
about unimportant details, like the price of ice cream or
the speed limit in California. This should lead up to the
climax in which no words are necessary and which must
come out perfect."

I lowered my eyes. "Okay."

But he went on with the lecture and I had only myself
to blame; I should have known better than to tell him the
truth. Once he started on his favorite subject, there was no
shutting him up.

"You have no sense of timing and that's bad. And you
don't see the whole act, just the separate scenes. I've read
that Marlon Brando said an actor has to also be a poet.
There's wisdom in that. Brando is always in command of all
the material and it shows. The principle you have to base
your performance on is very simple, really; if you're locked
up in a dark room, you become accustomed to the darkness
after awhile. But if someone keeps turning the light on and
off, your suffering is unbearable, because each time you've
got to get used to the light and darkness. That's why when
you tell her you won't go to America you have to follow
with a period of peace, of quiet. You're both aware that the
problem remains, but you're afraid to broach it so as not
to hurt each other's feelings. It's like the moment of quiet
before a storm, a silence terrible to bear. Haven't you ever
read books about the sea and sailors?"

"No," I said. "As a kid I only read Ken Maynard's adven-
tures, slim paperbacks which we devoured in class, hidden
under our desks."

"Where did you go to school?"

"In Warsaw. A school run by nuns," I added quickly, eager to change the subject. "I was a lousy student. One nun
came up with the idea of making a dunce cap and I had to

wear it for almost four years."

"She must have been a sadist."

"All of them were. When the bishop of Warsaw diocese died, the kids from Catholic schools had to go and pray for him. There he was, laid out in state, one gloved hand hanging limply from the open coffin, and we had to kneel down and kiss that cold, rigid hand. When my turn came, I said I won't do it, and the nuns dragged me over by force. So I bit into that dead hand with such a fury that it took several nuns to pry me off. They almost overturned the coffin."

"How old were you?"

"I don't remember. Maybe nine."

"It's a good story," Robert said. "Tell it to that broad. Americans love analyzing experiences like that. Let her exercise her brains. A small thing, but what joy it can bring to a woman! Just like a prick."

THE MAN RETURNED WITH HIS DOG, A BOXER. BOTH OF them looked like cheats. Robert started bargaining with the man while I played with the dog. It was very thin; we knew we'd have to fatten it up before going to Tiberias. The problem was we had no place to cook. Oh well, I thought, we can always move back to the hotel on Allenby Street and borrow an electric hot plate from somebody. Maybe even Harry would agree to cook meals for the dog if we paid him extra.

"What's it called?" I asked.

"Call it anything you like," the man answered. "It's yours."

"Not yet," Robert said. "We haven't bought it yet. This isn't a dog, it's skin and bones. What have you been feeding it? Barbiturates?"

"This is a purebred. Purebreds shouldn't be fat. Just like good fighting cocks."

"We'll pay you eighty pounds for the dog, but you'll have to keep it three or four days longer. Here, fifty pounds in advance, but be sure you take good care of it."

"Who said I'd sell it for eighty pounds?"

"I did."

They started arguing again. I turned away and studied the street. There was everything a man could ever need: army Willys, mules, girls, soldiers, Arabs, whites; the street smelled of hot copper and spicy foods, mules, hair cream, sea breeze, and gas; now, at six in the evening, the shadow of two slim minarets fell across it. I regretted Robert was about to wind up the deal and we would have to get back on the crowded bus and return to Tel Aviv. It would have been so much more enjoyable to stay on in the cafe, order beer, and wait until dusk, when the shadows of the slim minarets would fade and vanish and the charred sky would cover the earth with blackness.

Surprisingly, though, the bus wasn't crowded; apart from Robert and me, there were only several workers, and they fell asleep right away. The driver sped along the narrow streets, then turned toward the sea; at last we felt the fresh breeze that always begins just before the tide. The smell of copper, mules, and hair cream disappeared. The sea looked cool and bright. The first stars emerged. It crossed my mind that in prayers in Poland to the Holy Virgin, she is often called "the Morning Star." I asked Robert whether it could possibly be because another name for the star which shines the longest is the Star of Hope, but he told me to think of Tiberias instead and to find a good name for the dog.

"Its name must be as powerful as thunder," he said. "The dog appears on the scene, barks twice, we call out its name, and suddenly everything falls into place. Think of how Dostoyevsky named his characters. Take Dmitry Karamazov. That name is dynamite. There's strength in it, there's truth about human nature, there's everything you can wish for."

"What do you know about the girl in Tiberias?"

"She's a divorcée. It'll work out fine. Her husband turned out not to be the strong, virtuous man she had hoped to marry. He failed to fulfill her dreams and was blind to her sensitive nature. That's why she plunged into an affair with her chauffeur, and when he'd had enough and wanted to back out, she threatened to fire him and spill the goods on him to his wife. The chauffeur had a mental breakdown and ended up in a psychiatric clinic; the woman's husband had to pay the bills. And now you'll walk into her life."

"Bullshit," I said. "Who can afford a chauffeur in America these days?"

"Her husband is nearsighted. He can't watch movies or

read books. And he didn't pay the chauffeur full wages. Don't worry."

"I wish this would end. Why did I have to be born so goddamn poor?"

"And me?"

The bus slowed down. "Your stop," the driver called out to us over his shoulder.

We got out.

"I know what we can name the dog," I said to Robert.

"What?"

"Loser. It'll be like a paradoxical reaction. The last time I was in the hospital there were some patients who were trying to kick their addiction to sleeping pills. They suffered terribly. To fall asleep, just before bedtime, they had to drink giant mugs of strong black coffee. It's what the doctors call a paradoxical reaction. It'll be the same with the new dog. It's fine looking, it'll eat for two, so the name should work. What do you think?"

"Okay. From time to time you'll allude to the dog when you're talking to her. Subtly, of course. I'll tell you how."

"Sure," I said. "You know best."

In the evening we sat down to dinner: Robert, me, and little Johnny. A sickening family atmosphere prevailed in this hotel; I had to pass the time of day with these loafers and participate in conversations about food, the weather, and the beauty of the land. It was simply awful; Robert was much better at small talk. He could discuss any topic for hours.

"Where's your mom?" I asked the kid.

"Go to hell," he said, then added: "She's making herself look beautiful. As if you didn't know." He turned to Robert. "Has he always been this dumb?"

Robert interrupted the conversation he was having with some old geezer who, by the looks of him, should have long been dead. "Yes, my dear?" Robert asked.

"Nothing," Johnny said. "You're just as dumb as he is."

The guests at the next table burst out laughing. I flushed red and got up abruptly, walked over to the elevator, and pressed the button. Someone from the next table, a man in his early fifties with the contented look of a gangster who has made enough money to give up crime and turn into an honest citizen, joined me at the elevator.

"That kid sure made a fool of you," he said.

"Is that what you think?" I pushed him into the elevator and walked up the stairs. I opened the door to her room; she was sitting on the bed with an unlit cigarette in her hand.

"Don't you feel well?" I asked.

"Not really."

"What's wrong?"

"Nothing. Except Johnny's father is coming here tonight."

"How do you know?"

"He called to ask whether it'd be okay. I told him yes."

"It'll turn out fine, don't worry. Light your cigarette and come downstairs with me."

"You think it will?"

"I'm certain."

"You don't know what it means to Johnny to actually meet his father. It's all my fault, of course. It was me who kept telling him how wise and strong his daddy was; I said everything he wanted to hear. And now he believes everything I told him and expects to meet some superman."

"I don't see how you can change that at this point."

"I know. But Johnny is too young to understand. He's expecting a strong, wonderful stranger to come up to him and say: 'John, my son, I'm your daddy.'"

"And what's your ex-husband really like?"

"I'm not sure. But he's not what Johnny's been dreaming about." Suddenly she burst into tears and cried just like that time on the beach, hopelessly and unobtrusively, as a child might. "I didn't want Johnny to suffer. Or feel unloved. What else could I do?"

"Come on, let's go," I said. "It'll be okay."

She looked up at me and smiled. "You really think so?"

"Remember, I'll be there. And so will Uncle Robert. And the dog."

We went downstairs. The reformed gangster I had met at the elevator sent me a murderous look. I sat down.

A strange calm descended over me, as it sometimes does. As soon as the man walked into the dining room, I knew what was going to happen. He recognized me immediately: it was that poor wino who had asked Robert for a beer and who I'd chased away. He was more drunk than before and there was a foolish grin on his face; he must have wanted to muster up his courage. Then he saw me; I had no doubt what he'd do. As the memory of our previous meetings stirred in his unhappy, intoxicated mind, his grin vanished. He came up to us, bumping into the waiter serving soup to the guests sitting at the next table; the soup landed right in their laps.

"You whore," he said to her.

I got up. "Is that the way to greet a lady?" I asked.

"Whore," he said again.

She clutched my hand.

We looked at each other, and at that moment he must have understood everything. It became very quiet. He hit me in the face and two women screamed. I grabbed him by the throat, but then I saw the expression on the kid's face. He was watching me, pale and frightened; his nose wrinkled like a dog's, his upper lip curled, showing his teeth.

I didn't say anything, just pushed the drunk away, or, rather, let go of him, and he staggered and almost fell. A deep silence descended over the room. I started walking toward the door, tossing away a napkin I had unconsciously picked up from the table. When the door slammed behind me, pandemonium broke out.

Robert caught up with me on the stairs. His face was

pale and covered with sweat.

"Now," he said. "Don't wait, do it now. Everything came out beautifully, it'll be just perfect."

"No, not today," I said. "Tomorrow."

He kissed my hand; I could feel his lips trembling. "You were wonderful, magnificent! But don't wait, do it now. Tomorrow won't be the same."

"Okay."

We went into the room. Robert took out the pistol from our suitcase and started loading it. His hands were shaking. I walked up to the window and gazed at the sea. Robert kept talking, but I wasn't listening. I was watching our dog run around on the beach; some kids were chasing it, and it was barking loudly.

"Ready," Robert announced.

I turned around and took the pistol from him.

"Just don't hit me too hard," he said.

"Did I ever hit you too hard?"

"No. You were fantastic, fantastic. Let's go."

"I want to look at the sea again."

"There's no time."

We started going down the stairs. At the bottom landing I broke into a run; Robert followed me with great strides.

"It's madness!" he screamed. "Stop him!"

I was supposed to hit him, but I only pushed him away. I crossed the dining room and ran out to the beach. There was a strong wind blowing, so the beach was practically deserted. I whistled, and Spot began running toward me in huge leaps; I pulled the trigger, firing several times in rapid succession, but I didn't manage to empty the gun. The dog lay sprawled at my feet. It must have been dead after the second or third shot. I threw the gun next to the body and went back to my room.

Three vials of Nembutal were waiting for me on the table. I took the glass of water Robert had prepared for me and started swallowing the pills. Robert was scribbling something; drops of perspiration fell onto the sheet of paper.

"What are you writing?" I asked.

"'Pray for my soul,'" he said.

"Better write: 'Forgive me my sins and pray for my miserable soul.' And maybe add: 'None of you ever truly liked me, nor did I ever truly like any of you.'"

"No. Only this: 'Pray for my soul.' It's more forceful."

I stretched out on the bed and said, "Leave me now."

"Do you feel anything?"

"Not yet. But I will soon. Go away."

He stood hesitating.

"Go away," I said again.

"Okay. So long, son. In two days' time it'll be all over. Don't worry."

He left. I knew I would feel a rocking for a while, and I did. I was being carried by some dark and gentle wave, but I didn't fall asleep yet. I knew the next moment would be the worst; I always dreaded it.

I was no longer in a cheap and ugly hotel room. I was no longer carried by a gentle wave. I was walking along a country road and I could see in the distance, in the middle of an empty field, a girl with her back to me; I could see her long hair, her beautiful slender legs and her tanned shoulders. She was bending over something hidden from my sight, which I knew I would never see. Then I suddenly found myself back in my bed in the tastelessly decorated hotel room, but in the next moment I was looking at the girl's graceful figure again. I knew I would see her face now.

"Don't be shy," I said aloud. "I'm coming to you."

She turned to me, and I saw her face, old and ugly, then she smiled, exposing her rotten teeth. I could even smell her awful, stinking breath. I knew I was already on the other side of the hill.

ON THE THIRD DAY IT WAS ALL OVER. I WAS LYING ON THE terrace of a small, elegant hotel, pretending to be asleep. It was very quiet because everybody was resting after dinner, so I had no trouble hearing what Robert was telling her. I knew his text almost by rote, but I enjoyed listening to him all the same.

"At least he'll have enough sleep," Robert said. "He often suffers from insomnia."

"What do you think? Should I leave now?" she asked. "I'm afraid he may feel embarrassed when he wakes up."

"He should," Robert said, and I knew there was a stern look on his face, just as if he were playing the part of an Indian chief sending somebody to his death. "It's no joke. Whatever one does, one has to try to do it right."

"Don't be so cruel."

"Poor, stupid loser. He even failed to take his own life."

"He would have died if you hadn't gone back to the room," she said.

"Yes, that was sheer luck. I'd forgotten to take my passport and I needed it the next day. I didn't want to wake the two of you in the morning."

They both fell silent for a moment.

"That poor dog was all he had," Robert said. "I don't know why he shot it. Maybe he had to get his anger out after your husband hit him. So he shot the dog."

"He shouldn't have done it."

"Thank God he did!"

"Why?"

"Because he fired all the bullets he had, so he couldn't

shoot himself. All that remained were those stupid sleeping pills."

"To kill himself because of that worthless drunk!"

"No. It was because your son was present. The kid saved his father. Jacob didn't want to hit him because of the kid."

"I know. Someday Johnny'll understand."

"Write to him," Robert said. "He'll be happy to hear from you."

"Write?"

"Yes. Send the letter to me and I'll forward it to him."

"But he's coming with me!"

"I'm afraid you don't know him," Robert said.

"Listen, there's something wrong here. Something I don't understand. Why does he have to go to Australia to work? Why can't he come to America with me and try to find a job there? I don't get it, Bobby."

"It's simple. He's scared."

"Of what?"

"I don't know if I can tell you."

"Bobby, you're the only friend he has. If you won't help me, who will? Bobby, please!"

"His isn't a romantic story, it's a sad one," Robert said. "Have you seen the picture of an old lady in his room?"

"You mean his mother?"

"Yes," Robert said, and I remembered the snapshot of the bouncer's mom. "She was very ill and he had to go into debt to send her money for the hospital and the operation. Unfortunately, it didn't do much good. She died."

"Oh, the poor man," she whispered, and the image of my real mother, who is in perfect health and swills vodka like a hussar flashed through my mind.

"He can't leave Israel without his passport, and it's held by the lawyer representing the people he borrowed money from. When he told the lawyer he found employment in Australia and showed him his contract, the lawyer agreed to return the passport. But the arrangement is that Jacob's Australian employer will regularly deduct part of his pay and send it directly to the creditors. Do you see it all now?"

"Why can't he send them money from the States?"

"Because he's a Pole, dear," Robert said, "and he'd have to wait six to eight years for an immigration visa. He can go to the States as a tourist only. And to go as a tourist you need money."

"How much does he owe those people?"

"Two thousand three hundred eighty dollars."

"Do you mean to tell me he wanted to kill himself for two thousand dollars?"

"I didn't say that was the reason. I can only guess what went on in his mind. He finally managed to find a job and then he met you. He didn't want to go to Australia anymore, only to the States with you. But that goddamn lawyer wouldn't let him have his passport. Next your husband showed up and hit him in the face, and he couldn't hit him back because of your kid. So he shot the dog and his mind went crazy. I don't know what really happened. You're the one who should know." His voice was stern and hard.

After a moment, she asked softly, "Why, Bobby? Why do you think I should know?"

"Because he loves you," Robert replied in the same stern voice. "And you love him."

"Will you hate me if I take him away?"

"No. It's me who's a loser. I don't hate anybody." He paused and said again, "Yes, I'm a loser."

"Do you know how to straighten things out with that lawyer?"

"He has to go to him and pay off his debts."

"Oh, God, he won't do it. He won't take money from me."

Robert was silent for a long while, then he laughed.

"What are you laughing at, Bobby?"

"At myself. We've been friends for so long and gone through so much together. And yet the only thing I can do for him is to help him leave, even though it means I'll never see him again. Isn't that something? But I'll do it."

Neither of them said a word for a while. I couldn't see the sea from the terrace, but I could hear the waves. They had kicked us out of the hotel, and we were all staying in a small inn owned by a German Jew, a calm, elderly gentleman with well-groomed hands. Robert had brought me there from the hospital earlier in the day. He had to sign a statement that the patient was being released at his own request and against medical advice. And so here I was, and next to my bed was a vase full of flowers. I amused myself by imagining Robert's expression when he bought them for me.

"Will you make us some coffee, Bobby?" she said.

"Okay, but if you want, we can go downstairs for coffee."

"Bobby, I still don't understand why he shot his dog."

"I don't know," he said. "I think he intended to destroy everything he possessed. Or maybe he wanted to make the parting with you easier for himself? I don't know. The dog was his. It was all he had."

"I'm wondering how to explain it to Johnny. You know, Bobby, that all Americans love dogs?"

"Tell him Spot was ill and had to be shot. In Westerns cowboys often shoot their horses and everybody thinks that's all right. When he grows up, you can tell him Jacob shot the dog because he was in love with you and thought he'd have to leave you. So he shot the dog to appear cruel and stupid. So you wouldn't have to suffer, you know."

"Is that true, Bobby?"

"Let's go and have coffee," he said.

"Why am I so dumb?" she cried. "Why didn't I think of it myself? He killed the dog because he wanted me to stop loving him, didn't he, Bobby?"

"Let's go have that coffee."

"I should have thought of it myself."

"You'll have lots of time to think it all through," he said. "I can promise you that. Come on, let's go. I need that coffee."

I turned over and went to sleep.

THEY WERE LEAVING THE NEXT DAY. AFTER BREAKFAST I rang for a taxi and picked up her suitcase to carry it down to the lobby.

"No," she said, taking it out of my hand. "You're still too weak."

"I won't say good-bye to you," I said.

"Why not?"

"There's a saying that welcomes are nicer than farewells."

She stood in front of me, smiling, then she turned and climbed into the waiting cab. "John would like to speak to you," she said through the window.

"Will it be very painful?"

"Who knows?"

I turned; the kid was standing behind me, solid as a rock. Robert was arguing with the taxi driver over the fare.

"You want to talk to me?" I asked.

"Yes," Johnny said. "But not here. Let's go somewhere."

We moved away from the cab. But he didn't say anything; he just stared gloomily at his sneakers.

"What's the problem, Johnny?"

"Listen," he said, jerking up his head, "I know you could have smashed my daddy to bits."

"Is that so?"

"I know you could have made him spit chalk. And I know why you didn't."

"Did your mom tell you?"

"Nobody had to tell me anything. I'm not dumb. Mom didn't tell me anything, by the way."

"Okay. Consider the matter closed. Thank you, John."

But he hadn't finished yet. I saw tears in his eyes; I knelt down and embraced him, and he threw his arms around my neck.

"I'd like to ask you something," he said.

"Go ahead, ask anything you want."

"When you come to the States, can I call you Daddy?"

"Sure," I said. "You can start calling me that now."

He left, and as soon as he climbed into the cab, it drove away. Precisely at this moment the bouncer appeared, as suddenly as if he had emerged from under the ground. I'll never know where he had been hiding so well that nobody saw him, neither Robert, me, nor her. He was beaming; he looked like a potato gifted with intelligence.

"Okay," he said. "Now we can settle our accounts."

He and Robert sat down; so did I, but I didn't listen to them. A group of young women in uniform were walking down HaYarkon Street singing. I watched them for a while, and then turned back to the two men. When I did this, my share of the money was waiting for me; I pocketed the bills without counting. Robert and the bouncer were arguing again about an earlier deal.

"Where did you go?" Robert asked.

"I went to see J."

"J knew nothing of this scheme. I told you to go see G."

"I won't let you order me around."

"And I won't let you swindle me."

I remembered it was time to collect our new dog, and since Robert's squabbles usually bored me, I decided to leave him with the bouncer and go to Jaffa by myself. I knew how much Robert enjoyed arguing; now I also knew about the bouncer. As I was slowly walking down HaYarkon Street, it crossed my mind that in fact I knew the whole city, the whole country. I passed a nightclub, which was closed this time of day. I knew the black man who played drums there; I thought of his drums covered with dust until evening when his quick fingers would bring them to life with the beat of a song. I passed a small hotel where a queer who was in love with me worked as a desk clerk; whenever I wanted to get money from him, I would cut my face with a razor blade and make him watch. I did this when I was really broke.

I knew many places and many people here. Why couldn't I write about them? Why could I feel so much but not be able to put it down in writing? I don't know. Why haven't I ever said or written that there is no greater misery than living without awareness of God, contrary to His commandments? I don't know. And why haven't I ever said that the worst sin is to betray the love of another human being? I don't know. Maybe it was too hot for such profound statements, or maybe I've forgotten. I had seven hundred American dollars and over a hundred pounds in my pockets. In Israel, seven hundred dollars is a lot of money. And I expected to score some more in Tiberias. I'd be able to rent a separate room for myself, buy lots of books, and read them; evenings I'd go to the cheap movie theater on Ben Yehudah Street, and late at night I'd listen to the rain fall on the city. And so it would be till spring. Until spring I wouldn't have to talk of love to anybody; till spring I wouldn't have to hustle any more broads. But why did I have to be poor, why wasn't I born in some rich bastard's bed? If I were rich, I could live in solitude among millions of people and share their joys instead of only their exhaustion. Nothing will ever change for me.

I had to get that goddamn boxer. On the corner of HaYarkon, a poor man sat who made his living shining shoes. I walked up to him, sat down, and watched his old hands polish my shoes. When he finished, I pulled out a pound note, rolled it into a ball, and tossed it to him.

"God bless you, mister," he said. "You're a good man."

"I like that," I said. I took another pound note from my pocket, rolled it into a ball and threw it at him. He looked up at me expectantly. "I like what you said," I told him. "In about an hour I'll be coming back this way with a dog. When you see me, say that again, okay?"

COCAINE BY PITIGRILLI

Paris in the 1920s – dizzy and decadent. Where a young man can make a fortune with his wits ... unless he is led into temptation. Cocaine's dandified hero Tito Arnaudi invents lurid scandals and gruesome deaths, and sells these stories to the newspapers. But his own life becomes even more outrageous when he acquires three demanding mistresses. Elegant, witty and wicked, Pitigrilli's classic novel was first published in Italian in 1921 and retains its venom even today.

THE MISSING YEAR OF JUAN SALVATIERRA BY PEDRO MAIRAL

At the age of nine, Juan Salvatierra became mute following a horse riding accident. At twenty, he began secretly painting a series of canvases on which he detailed six decades of life in his village on Argentina's frontier with Uruguay. After his death, his sons return to deal with their inheritance: a shed packed with rolls over two miles long. But an essential roll is missing. A search ensues that illuminates links between art and life, with past family secrets casting their shadows on the present.

FANNY VON ARNSTEIN: DAUGHTER OF THE ENLIGHTENMENT BY HILDE SPIEL

In 1776 Fanny von Arnstein, the daughter of the Jewish master of the royal mint in Berlin, came to Vienna as an 18-year-old bride. She married a financier to the Austro-Hungarian imperial court, and hosted an ever more splendid salon which attracted luminaries of the day. Spiel's elegantly written and carefully researched biography provides a vivid portrait of a passionate woman who advocated for the rights of Jews, and illuminates a central era in European

SOME DAY BY SHEMI ZARHIN

On the shores of Israel's Sea of Galilee lies the city of Tiberias, a place bursting with sexuality and longing for love. The air is saturated with smells of cooking and passion. Some Day is a gripping family saga, a sensual and emotional feast that plays out over decades. This is an enchanting tale about tragic fates that disrupt families and break our hearts. Zarhin's hypnotic writing renders a painfully delicious vision of individual lives behind Israel's larger national story.

THE GOOD LIFE ELSEWHERE BY VLADIMIR LORCHENKOV

The very funny - and very sad - story of a group of villagers and their tragicomic efforts to emigrate from Europe's most impoverished nation to Italy for work. An Orthodox priest is deserted by his wife for an art-dealing atheist; a mechanic redesigns his tractor for travel by air and sea; and thousands of villagers take to the road on a modern-day religious crusade to make it to the Italian Promised Land. A country where 25 percent of its population works abroad, remittances make up nearly 40 percent of GDP, and alcohol consumption per capita is the world's highest – Moldova surely has its problems. But, as Lorchenkov vividly shows, it's also a country whose residents don't give up easily.

To purchase these titles and for more information please visit newvesselpress.com.

New Vessel Press